GETTING THE GIRL

OTHER NOVELS BY SUSAN JUBY:

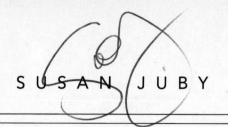

SUSAN JUBY

GETTING THE GIRL

A Guide to Private Investigation,
Surveillance, and Cookery

HarperTrophy Canada™
An imprint of HarperCollins Publishers Ltd

Getting the Girl
Copyright © 2008 by Susan Juby.
All rights reserved.

Published by HarperTrophyCanada™, an imprint of
HarperCollins Publishers Ltd.

Originally published by HarperTrophyCanada™
in a trade paperback edition: 2008
This digest edition: 2010

HarperTrophyCanada™ is a trademark of
HarperCollins Publishers.

HarperCollins books may be purchased for educational,
business, or sales promotional use through our
Special Markets Department.

HarperCollins Publishers Ltd
2 Bloor Street East, 20th Floor
Toronto, Ontario, Canada
M4W 1A8

www.harpercollins.ca

Library and Archives Canada Cataloguing in Publication
Juby, Susan, 1969–
Getting the girl : a guide to private investigation, surveillance, and
cookery / Susan Juby.

ISBN 978-1-55468-676-6

I. Title.
PS8569.U324G48 2009   JC813'.6   C2009-905800-6

Printed and bound in the United States
HC 9 8 7 6 5 4 3 2 1

For my brothers, Trevor, Aaron, and Scott

Acknowledgments

Many thanks to my trusted readers
who vetted the manuscript, Bill Juby,
Wendy Banta, Aaron and Scott Banta,
Stephanie Dubinsky, Susin Nielson, and,
as always, my editors Ruth and Lynne,
my agent, Hilary, and my husband, James.

Mack daddy is used in some other senses parallel to extended senses of mack. One is "a good-looking man; a ladies' man; playboy." Another is "a person, especially a man, who is influential, intelligent, successful, etc."

—The Urban Dictionary

There is no man alive who is not partially jackass. When we detect some areas of jackassery within ourselves, we feel discontent. Our image suffers.

—Meyer to Travis McGee in *A Tan and Sandy Silence* by John D. MacDonald

Part I
FRYING PAN

OCTOBER

ON THE BLEACHERS

LUNCHTIME

I was sitting on the old blue bleachers with Dini. It was just the two of us. Alone. Together. It's not hard to find Dini Trioli alone because she's got this well-developed deep and artistic side that causes her to spend a lot of time by herself. I was waiting for her to stop chewing so I could make my move.

We had a perfect view of the Goths who smoke down at the far edge of the athletics field. I figure the Goths using the edge of the sports field as their smoking area is probably some kind of statement on how they feel about school sports. I can dig that. A lot of people feel the same way. Take me, for example. I'm always picked third from last. Second to last is Bailey Farber, who has only one and a half legs. The guy usually picked last is my friend Rick, who has ultrasensitive pain receptors, which make sports difficult for him. Or so he says.

I've also heard that if you pay close attention, which I always do, you can sometimes spot one of the Defiled wandering back and forth like a ghost at the very edge of school property.

It's my second month at Harewood Technical. Before I came here I was worried about going into ninth grade. High school in general has a reputation for suckage and I had heard that this high school takes the popularity thing to a whole new level.

See, at Harewood Technical you have your usuals—jocks, Trophy Wives, scholars—but there's also this whole other class of people called the Defiled. They aren't just unpopular—they are basically invisible.

Only girls get defiled at Harewood Tech and so most of the girls from my old school, Harmack Junior High, were freaking out before school started, which I can understand.

I first remember hearing about the defilings at Harewood Tech when I was in fifth grade, although no one knows who started defiling or how long it's been going on.

When a girl gets defiled, her picture, with a *D* written over it, is posted on the mirrors of all the student bathrooms. It's like an official notice that she's crossed the line of no social return. At first, people say terrible things about why the girl got defiled, like that she's nasty or skanky or a slut or whatever. After a day or so of that, people start to ignore her. Not in a not-noticing way, but more in an *erasing* way. No one will talk to her or even look at her except the teachers, and from what I heard, even they mostly avoid the Defiled.

No one knows who decides who is going to be defiled. Some people think the Defiler is one person, other people think defiling is the work of a shadowy committee. So far, though, defiling seems like one of those things that kids in elementary school make up to freak themselves out about high school.

It was tense at first, though. I mean, most eighth graders getting ready to move to high school worry about how hard the work will be and whether they'll have any friends, but the girls in my class were nervous about getting defiled. It made me feel bad for them, which is why I offered to give them all free back rubs on the last day of eighth grade and on our first day at Harewood. None of them took me up on my generosity, but I know they appreciated the way I'm always looking out for them. I'm pretty much always looking out for the ladies. I guess you could say I'm thoughtful.

It's been over a month now and everyone seems to have relaxed. None of the girls from my old school have been defiled and neither has anyone else, so I'm free to focus on my real interest, which is getting with older ladies, which brings me back to Dini, tenth-grade goddess. I think the whole defiling thing might have been exaggerated. It just doesn't seem like that big a deal. Well, it probably is for the defiled people, but I still haven't seen one of those yet. Other than that, the school seems okay.

Dini kept nibbling on her sandwich. I could see the little green alfalfa sprouts poking out from the sides of the whole-wheat bread. She seems like a very healthy eater, which explains her skin, which is awesome, even though she's older. I was having fries and gravy from the Pirate Chips truck that parks on the street near the school. My skin probably looked like I had been stowed away on a boat for six months without proper food, water, or sun.

Maybe I shouldn't have gotten the fries. Dini didn't say anything, but I bet they grossed her out. I should have known that the combination of trans fats and meat-based gravy would be a turnoff.

I noticed Dini right away on the first day of school. Last Tuesday at lunch I took a chance and offered to buy her a hamburger. It was the first time I spoke to her. She told me she doesn't eat anything with a face. Somewhere, back in the fogs of time, the gravy slopped all over these fries must have had a face. Sure, it was the face of a gravy packet or a large mother MSG. But it was still a face. Fries are not good will-you-go-out-with-me food.

I slid the fries to the side and hoped the wind would blow the smell away from her.

"Hey, so there's probably a dance coming up sometime this year."

Dini nodded, giving me wide eyes to make up for the fact that she couldn't answer because she was chewing. She chews nicely. With her mouth closed and everything.

"I hate dances," I said.

Dini raised an eyebrow and swallowed her bite.

"I mean, I hate most dances. The whole . . . music and dancing thing. With teachers. Parents. Chaperones. Watching. The way I see it, dancing should be private."

Dini still didn't say anything. I tried not to stare as she took another bite of her sandwich. I once read that Hollywood celebrities are afraid to eat in case someone takes a picture of them doing it and they look like pigs, or at least like people who eat. Dini wouldn't have that problem. I bet people would buy tickets to see her eat. I know I would.

"Unless you're dancing with a friend. Then dances are okay. I'm speaking now as an expiring dancer myself."

She swallowed and her throat moved. There was a sesame seed stuck to her lip. Most people, you'd want to tell them "Hey, you've got something on your face." Me, I just wished I *was* that seed.

"You mean aspiring dancer."

"Okay. But as I was saying, if you were interested, we could go to a dance together sometime. I bet you've got a few moves that you could teach me. You know, the twirl with hands raised, the twirl with hands at sides, the twirl with arms outstretched."

Dini laughed. "The twirls only work if you're wearing a long skirt or a skirt over pants," she said.

"I'm up for it if you are."

She smiled at me, about to say yes, even though I have only talked to her twice and I am younger than she is and not exactly tall. Her eyes were vegetarian blue, the whites perfectly white and bright.

My heart was racing like a greyhound, but before she could say yes, this voice came booming out of nowhere.

"This guy bothering you?"

Lester Broadside stood beside the bleachers. His face was at my shoe level but he still looked taller than me.

Lester Broadside, aka Lester the Molester. Eleventh grader. One of the most popular guys at Harewood Tech. Famous for his hair, which is long and hangs in his eyes in this cool way. He has a slightly crooked smile that he probably practices making in the bathroom mirror. He's captain of the lacrosse team. Mr. Big Man on Campus. I could forgive all that, but the guy's an assweed, especially where girls are concerned. You can see it in his eyes.

But the girls don't notice. Girls never do.

Right in front of my eyes, Dini turned pod. She smiled at Lester and kind of shrank into herself. She literally got smaller. It was horrible to watch.

"You ready for that ride now?" he asked her.

I looked around, half expecting to see him holding a unicorn or something. That's how special he made the ride sound.

"Now?" she said, all shy. Like she couldn't believe her good luck.

"Let's go," he said. He put a hand on the bleacher. Just rested it there. The bleacher looked grateful.

Dini gave me a little sideways look and I knew it was all over. "I'll see you later, Sherm?" she said, uptalking at the end of her sentence.

I nodded and it was my turn to swallow.

She stepped down from the bleacher, moving real careful, like she was in front of a big audience, like this is the one time in her life she wanted to make sure not to trip and fall. Like she was walking up the aisle at her wedding.

It was the walk that got me.

always lending me her books. What I've noticed is that the detectives in her books and the ones on TV ignore their women quite a bit because they are quite consumed by their investigations. They are sort of jerks, in fact. So using my powers of reasoning, I thought maybe all you need to do to get a woman to do what you want is ignore her, but so far that hasn't worked for me. I've tried. I've ignored almost every girl in my class at one time or another and not one of them has noticed. I've gone whole days not speaking to my mother when I was trying to get something from her. But my mother doesn't care, either. She just keeps talking to me the same way some people talk to their pets.

"Hello, sweet 'ums," she'll say, and follow that up with a bunch of baby talk. Sometimes I worry that my mother may be trying to make me gay. It's not just the baby talk. It's our entire living environment. My mother is into glitter. This is very damaging for a developing male. My friend Ashton says our house looks like a stripper named Cherry Rider should live in it. We rent an old house right on the edge of Harewood in the south end of town, which some people call Scarewood, because it's not too wealthy or anything. But even though parts of our neighborhood are kind of rough, our house looks as girly as it's possible for a house to look, at least on the inside. My mother has painted all the walls a glossy red, except my bedroom, which I convinced her to leave off-white.

Most of the pictures on the walls are of overweight, old-fashioned ladies wearing what is basically underwear. I am quite mature, considering I'm the youngest guy in my class, but it's hard to underestimate the negative effect this art is probably having on my sexual development. We have thirty-four throw pillows and every doorway has a beaded curtain. We only have one very small TV hidden behind a painted screen. I rarely get to watch the programs Vanessa recommends, such as *Law & Order*, *Law & Order: Criminal Intent*, and *Law & Order: Special Victims Unit*, because my mother is watching videotapes of herself dancing.

My mother is into *burlesque* dancing. It's like stripping, only not quite as naked. I know because I've watched all of her instructional videos several times. Most of the performers are on the bigger, jigglier side. Except my mom who is in her early thirties and probably hasn't even finished developing. My mom's burlesque dancing friends joke around and laugh a lot. They are like female drag queens.

My mother spends almost everything she earns on new costumes. Her real job, which is being a bartender, doesn't pay much, so not only are we poor, we also live in semisqualor. There is dust all over everything, not to mention fabric and feathers and bits of fake fur and fishnet stockings lying around.

I once told my mom that if Child Services got a look at our place, she'd have some explaining to do, but she just laughed and said there is a social worker in her burlesque troop, the Bawdville Revue, and that she can set up a meeting for me if I'd like.

"You have two choices growing up in a house like this," Ashton told me a while ago. He was sitting with his legs crossed on our zebra-patterned chaise lounge with the faded cranberry juice stain on the arm. "You're either going to be gay or a Peeping Tom."

Ashton is very open-minded, so I wasn't offended. But Rick was.

"Shut up, man. You're going to freak him out," he said, although he was the one who sounded freaked out. "Having a peeler for a mom is just going to help Sherm understand the ladies."

"My mom's not a peeler," I said. "She keeps some of her clothes on when she performs."

"Burlesque is descended from vaudeville," said Ashton. "It's extremely sexy."

Rick was right. I am very interested in girls. I actually study them. I am almost like a scholar of women. My friend Vanessa says I'm a scholar of stalking, but she's quite cynical, probably from all her crime reading which has given her an abnormally dark view of life.

My curiosity might come from growing up with an inappropriately youthful single mother. It's like we're nearly the same age. I am fourteen, the youngest guy in my class, thanks to a late fall birthday. And my mother *dresses* like a lot of fourteen-year-olds. Ones with bad self-esteem. I'm not trying to be critical. I'm only pointing out what other parents—

mothers, mostly—have been saying for years.

My mother had me when she was sixteen. She's a doctor's daughter and her getting pregnant in tenth grade by an unknown boy was not "part of the program." Things are still a bit tense between her and my grandparents. I try to act as a median, or whatever you call it, but sometimes I feel like I just get in the way.

Living with my mother and her dancing and dressing up and everything has been an education in the ways of womankind. I thought I knew a few things about girls—at least I did until I met Dini and Lester the Molester. Now I realize I don't know anything about women. Not Dini. Not my mom. Every woman is an island covered in fog and surrounded by rocks and riptides and a lot of other hazards.

Even the half-naked ladies in the prints in the bathroom are a complete mystery to me. I should know them inside and out, considering all the time I've spent staring at them and imagining what lies under their striped bloomers and wondering why their bras look so uncomfortable.

This afternoon I was in the bathroom thinking

about that exact subject when the phone rang.

"Sherman! Phone!" called my mom from the kitchen.

"I'm busy," I said.

"It's Rick!"

"I'll call him back," I said, but it was too late. The mood was ruined. I should never try and have personal time in the bathroom when my mother is home.

"Sherm, honey, hurry up. I've got to get to work."

I got myself reorganized and, avoiding the eyes of the ladies, left the bathroom.

My mother handed me the phone and gave me one of those looks she always gets when I spend too much time in the can. Like she thinks I'm funny and sad at the same time. I don't love that look, to be honest.

"Hey," I said into the receiver.

"Is for horses," said my mom, from her position near the toaster.

I frowned to show I would appreciate a bit of privacy, but she didn't notice.

"How'd it go? Did you ask her out?" asked Rick.

"Not exactly."

"What happened?"

"Nothing."

"Okay, Sherm. I've got my toast and I'm heading to work now. Don't stay up too late," said my mother.

I nodded and tried not to flinch when she kissed me because I'm practically a grown man and I was on the phone, for God's sake.

As the door shut behind her, Rick piped up again. "Hey," he said.

"Is for horses," I said.

"Shut up. Your mom gone?"

"Yeah."

"Is she going dancing?"

"No. She's working. And don't talk about her dancing, you pervert."

"Don't blow a ventricle. I'm just asking. Anyway, did you ask Dini out?"

"Yeah. But Lester came along right in the middle and took her for a car ride."

"Lester *Broadside*? Lester the Molester? What are you going to do?"

"What do you mean? Nothing. I'm done, man. Brad Pitt might as well have asked her out."

"You've got to do something. You don't want her to end up defiled, do you?"

"What?"

"That's what happened to the last girl who went out with Lester Broadside. He'd been dating her for about a month or so and *wham*! She got hit with the Big D. They say Broadside might *be* a Defiler. They say he defiled his own girlfriend to get rid of her."

"Who's they?"

"People."

"But nobody knows who the Defilers are."

"Seems like a pretty weird coincidence, though."

"Yeah, well, no one's going to defile Dini."

"Anyone can get defiled, dude. Girls, anyway."

"Not Dini," I said. I tried to sound confident, but when I hung up the phone I felt sick.

A THING OR TWO
ABOUT RHODODENDRONS

When a guy gets worried, it's important that he has a mature man to talk to. So the day after I talked to Rick I went to see my mentor. About a year ago my mom and my school counselor decided that I needed a mentor to make up for me not having a father. They picked our neighbor, Fred King, who moved next door after his marriage broke up. He lives in a nice green house with a garden all the way around. We live in a brown house with a brown lawn and a couple of dead fruit trees in the yard. My mom's not much for tilling the soil and all that. I think Fred agreed to be my mentor because he feels sorry for our lawn.

Plus, our trees make us look sort of down and out.

The main problem with Fred as a mentor is that he isn't very male. I'm not saying he's female or anything. He's just kind of neutral. He's a garden writer, and he told me pretty early on that he hasn't got the first clue how to model manhood for me, but that he knows a thing or two about describing a rhododendron. So we decided that he should be my general-interest support guy. Mostly what we do is eat. Fred's a wicked cook.

You'd think that Fred, being a hotshot gardener, would be unhappy about living next door to a place where the only plant life is the bacteria on the compost pile, but when I asked him about it he said that at least when people take the local garden tour they never end up at our house by mistake.

When I went to get his advice on the Dini situation I found him lying on his back in the living room. Fred's got a bad back from too much weeding, so he spends quite a bit of time lying on the floor, reading gardening books by English ladies with funny names like Hobhouse and Hogbelly and Wickerdick.

"Thank God you're here," said Fred as soon as I walked in. Our mentor-mentee relationship works both ways, I like to think.

"I need a drink. Would you please get me the bottle of Pimms from the fridge? My back's being particularly uncooperative today, and I can't face getting up."

Fred likes this drink with mint and Pimms in it. He's a big fan of all things British.

I got the Pimms and then he sent me out to his herb garden to get some mint. While I was out there I waved at my mom who was sitting over on our patch of desert, reading. She was shielded from the sun by a large black umbrella, her big black floppy hat, and giant black sunglasses. My mother is not a sunshine person.

"Took long enough," said Fred when I got back with his mint. He had gotten up and was sitting at the kitchen table with a pained look on his face. He took the leaves from me and sniffed them.

"Sherman, this is oregano."

"Sorry."

"It's okay. I can drink it without."

"I need some advice," I said. "About a girl."

Fred sipped at his drink and stared at the gardening book he'd been reading. "Can you believe this old cow is one of the most famous garden writers in the U.S.?"

Fred sometimes has difficulty tearing himself away from his reading.

"I think she's in danger."

"Must be sleeping with the publisher," Fred muttered.

"He's not a publisher. He's in eleventh grade. His name is Lester."

"Why else would she get the full-color treatment for this crap? Daylilies, daylilies, daylilies. Get a life, lady. Enough with the daylilies!"

Fred took another deep drink of his Pimms.

I waited for him to calm down.

"I'm sorry, Sherman. You were saying?"

"It's this girl I know. I'm sort of worried about her."

He waited for me to say more.

"She's been hanging around with this guy."

"Who is not you," said Fred, finally looking

up at me. A piece of hair had fallen away from his comb-over. Fred isn't very old, but he only has about eight strands of hair left on the top of his head. He does a lot with them, though.

"He's a bad guy. I don't trust him. I heard that sometimes bad things happen to the girls who go out with this guy."

I took a deep breath and decided to go all the way.

"In fact, the last girl who went out with him got kind of ruined," I said.

Fred froze with his glass halfway to his lips.

"Come again?" he said.

"It's this thing that happens at our school. Certain girls get, well, they get cast out. Their names and pictures are posted around school and people say that they did terrible things and after that no one talks to them. They're like lepers or pharaohs or something."

"I think you mean pariahs," said Fred. "And good Lord. That's terrible."

"Like I said, I'm worried about this girl. Because she's dating a guy whose last girlfriend got defiled."

Fred put his glass down on the book he'd just been reading.

SUSAN JUBY

"Defiled," he said. "That's quite a word."

I nodded.

He closed his eyes and leaned back his head.

Fred has never been one of your fast-acting mentors.

Finally he opened his eyes again.

"Maybe this girl and this fellow are just friends? And so she's not at risk of, uh, ruination at his hands?"

"I doubt it. He's not the kind of guy who's really friends with girls."

"How well do you know this girl?"

I shrugged. "Not that well. I've talked to her a couple of times. She's older. I like her."

"Maybe you should just come right out and tell her you're concerned about her."

I nodded again. He was right. Dini and I were friends, sort of. We'd had those two conversations. I jumped out of my chair.

"Thanks, Fred. See you later."

"Sherman, be careful, will you?" he said.

I nodded a third time. Fred looked kind of worried, but he may just have been irritated at the daylily lady.

GIRLS, GIRLS, GIRLS

You might wonder why I care so much about a girl I barely know, but you'd be missing the fact that I am concerned for the welfare of all ladies. Even old ones trying to cross the road and little ones on swing sets. I'm just very caring like that.

As I mentioned, I gave up on romancing girls my own age because, to be honest, they didn't seem ready for me. Also, my free hugs and massages campaign never really got off the ground with them. So I decided to move into the fast lane with the older girls at Harewood Tech. Figured I'd give them a chance for a piece of the Mack.

But none of them seemed too interested, either. The older girls seemed superbusy: walking around, talking to each other, being in class. I couldn't find an opening.

Until Dini. She's a tenth grader and I noticed right away that she hung out by herself a lot. At lunch she would either be in the art room or on the bleachers. Even though she's kind of a loner, she doesn't seem unhappy. She has this watchful vibe, like she's taking it all in but doesn't want to get involved.

When I first asked people about her, no one knew anything. She was like a mystery girl. I found out her name by looking at the labels on some of her work. The art room is full of her charcoal sketches, and her weird little sculptures of rabbits and deer that look a little bit like cartoons and a little bit like nightmares are displayed in the glass cases in the hallways. Personally, I've always felt close to loners. I'm actually sort of a loner myself, even though I have quite a few friends.

Plus, Dini is the perfect amount of girly. She's good-looking, but not so good-looking that you can't even look at her for fear of scorching your eyeballs. She smells good but not so good that she makes you sneeze. She isn't totally offended by everything you say—at least, she hasn't been offended by the things I've said to her in the two conversations we've had so far. She's athletic (I once saw her jog by our house), but not so athletic that she wears sweatpants all the time.

Now that I'm off girls my own age, I think Dini's my dream woman. Sure she's out of my league in a lot of ways, but I believe in aiming high. That's why I am not going to let Lester Broadside do anything to her.

I looked for Dini all the next day but didn't see her. She wasn't in her usual places. I thought I'd try and catch her on the way home. I was allowed to leave science class early that day because the girls at the table beside me dropped their beaker and sprayed me with the toxic liquid they created by accident. I would have screamed and run away, but that wouldn't have looked very manly, so I just smiled as the drops of science-gone-wrong burned their way through my clothes and into my skin.

"Go clean up," said Ms. Wuornos, who is young and attractive in a tired sort of way.

I had gym next period, so I went to the locker room to get changed. I checked out the holes in my shirt and the red marks on my skin. When I lifted my shirt I couldn't help but notice that my abs weren't exactly defined. I'm not fat, but there was no sign of muscle anywhere. Seriously. My body's like a pillow that has lost most of its stuffing. Maybe an old pillow that someone keeps their bone collection in.

I was thinking it was definitely time to bust a few sit-ups when I heard voices over in the next row of lockers.

"So, dude, did you tap that or what?"

"You know the Broadman's bagged her by now. You don't even have to ask," said another voice.

Curious, I crept over to the edge of my row of lockers and looked into the next aisle. Lester Broadside stood with his back to me. He was talking with two other guys. Lester had a towel around his waist and the rest of him was naked. He was built like a man. He wasn't having any problems with his middle looking like a mostly empty pillowcase.

"The longer the wait, the sweeter the prize,"

said one of the guys. He had on a black towel. He also looked like a man. One who competed in mixed martial arts.

"No, man, the saying is, the older the cherry, the sweeter the juice," said the third guy, who had on a pair of boxer briefs. He was, if anything, bigger than the other two.

"Shut up," said Lester Broadside.

"Is she older? Sweet," said black towel.

"No, man, she's younger. She's in tenth grade or something," said boxer briefs.

"It's not going to end up like the last time?" said black towel.

Lester didn't say anything. He pulled a white T-shirt over his head.

"Don't question the D," said boxer briefs. "Don't even think about it. Who cares what happens to them after you get done with them. Am I right or am I right?"

"Just drop it," said Lester finally.

I realized I was holding my breath as I walked backward to where my gym bag lay on the bench. When I finally let some air into my lungs I felt like I'd been underwater for an hour. Pains shot through my chest. I thought I might be having some kind of cardiac incident. They were talking trash about Dini! And unless I was mistaken, they were referring to defiling. I didn't know what to do.

A minute later the bell rang and the room started to fill up. I'm not sure if Lester and the two other guys were still in there or not. All I could hear was the blood sloshing around in my head. Next thing I knew the room was empty again and I was still sitting there.

"Sherman Mack. Get a move on. Now."

Coach Little, who has to be the most misnamed guy ever, stood glaring at me like a rhino about to charge.

I didn't move, because I was frozen in place.

"Mack, I'm telling you, get that butt in gear."

I tried to unclench my fists and put my hands on my knees.

"I don't feel good," I said.

"Do I look like I care how you feel?" asked Coach Little. "Let's go."

"I'm really not—"

"Like I said," said Coach Little. "Don't care."

I looked up at Coach and a red wave of anger

closed in. I was going to lose it.

"Uh, Coach Little?" said Rick, coming around the corner and taking in the situation.

"What, Santos?"

Rick was in his street clothes, sort of hunched over. He has a policy of never standing up straight in front of Coach Little in case Coach tries to make him participate in sports.

"I was wondering if you wanted me to watch today or if I should go to the library?"

Coach Little's shapeless face got even more shapeless. He bared his uneven yellowish teeth that were all angled slightly inward, like he'd had braces left on about five years too long.

"I don't care, Santos. You can watch the medicine ball drills or you can go read fairy stories in the library. Do whatever your *doctor* thinks will be safest."

"I'm a fantasy man, sir," said Rick. "Not into fairy tales."

Coach Little shook his head and his cauliflowered earlobes flapped. Behind him there was yelling in the gym. He turned to listen, then looked at us and growled. Like literally.

"*Rrrrr*," he said. "I gotta get out there. Mack, you better be over your problem and on that gym floor ready to throw some medicine balls around in five minutes or you can spend the rest of the period in the office. And you, Santos, go read or something. I don't want to look at you anymore."

Then he disappeared in that weirdly light-footed way he has.

Rick straightened up. "Sherm," he said. "Lucky I came along. It looked like you were about to lose your shit on Coach."

I shrugged.

"Are you crazy? If you freak out at Coach Little, you might get dead. The man's an animal."

I nodded. The problem is that when I lose it I also kind of lose the ability to make good judgment calls. I am similar to the Incredible Hulk in that way.

"What's up?" asked Rick, staring at me.

"Nothing."

I reached into the bottom of my bag for my balled-up gym shirt. It was stiff and crunchy. It smelled raunch.

"Come on. What happened?"

Of all my friends, Rick is the most sensitive, and I don't just mean his stomach. It's probably 'cause his parents make him go to confession at least once a week.

"Nothing. I heard Lester and some guys talking."

"Well?"

"I don't want to get into it."

"Come on. Was it about Dini?"

I didn't answer because I still wasn't sure what to make of what I'd heard.

"Did they mention defiling?" he asked.

When I still didn't say anything, he said, "Lester might be connected to the most powerful shadow organization in this school and be dating the woman you love and have killer hair, but the good news is, you have me on your crew. If you need me I'll be in the library."

I nodded and Rick limped away. He looked lame in both feet, which was sort of funny, because this week's doctor's note says he's got a pulled groin. After gym, I went to see if I could catch sight of Dini on the walk home.

5

ENJOYS WORKING WITH EGGS

Cooking is probably my favorite class so far in high school. To get into cooking at Harewood Tech you have to write an application essay where you talk about how you want to become a chef or a fry cook at the local grill or whatever. I wanted Rick to take the class with me, so I wrote his essay as well as my own. Mine was about the importance of a balanced diet for teenagers, so I basically made it up. In his I said he was interested in taking cooking because he loves working with eggs and was a morning person and might like to get a job at Smitties when he's older. I was just messing around, but Mrs. Samuels is one of those teachers who tries really hard and is always attempting to help Rick achieve his dream by assigning us complicated recipes with eggs, like crepes and frittatas. I don't mind because I'm pretty good with eggs, but Rick can't get past the fact that they are unfertilized chickens.

I convinced him to take the class with me by telling him that we'd get to eat what we cook, but it turns out that he doesn't really like eggs, and the stuff we cook isn't always too delicious anyway. Today we were making vegetarian omelets and, as usual, he was freaking out, especially when I told him to handle things for a few minutes.

"It's fine, man. Just keep an eye on things and I'll be back in a minute," I said.

"Sherm," said Rick, his voice high and squeaky, the way it gets when he's stressed. "You know I'm not into cooking, especially eggs."

I held up my hand in a masterful, cheflike way.

"Back in a second. I've got to talk to Vanessa."

"But you're the cooker! You're in charge! That was our deal! You promised!"

"Look, I have a lot going on right now. You're just going to have to handle things on your own for a second."

I walked over to Edna and Vanessa's kitchenette

and looked into their pan. "You guys need any help over here?"

Vanessa rolled her eyes, which are big and brown. "That's okay, Sherm. I think we can handle it." She looked over at Edna, who was leaning on the island, punching something into her BlackBerry. "At least, I can."

Vanessa and I have been friends since third grade. I have to admit that if I wasn't mostly an older-woman man these days, I'd probably have lustful feelings about her. Vanessa's a bigger girl, as in not thin. She's got that really smooth, soft-looking skin some plus-sized girls have. The other great thing about her is that she's quite relaxed, even when she's being extremely judgmental, which is often. You can enjoy being honest with Vanessa because she'll be honest right back. I think girls can tell when you appreciate things about them, such as their skin. Or the way their aprons fit.

I smiled at her, and then I smiled over at Edna, Vanessa's cooking partner, to try and get her involved in the nice over-the-omelet feeling the three of us had going. But Edna gave me this look like I was a total skeeze.

"I have another thing I wanted to talk to you about," I said to Vanessa.

"Oh?" Vanessa raised one of her eyebrows. "Let me guess—"

"Sherm!" Rick interrupted in his squeaky voice. "Can you please come take a look at this bitch, yo?"

When Rick gets stressed he sometimes tries to sound street to cover up the fact that he is basically shrieking like a girl. It doesn't work.

I ignored him.

"Look," I said to Vanessa. "There's this situation developing and I thought I'd run it by you."

Because she's so into detective novels and crime shows, Vanessa is always trying to get me to be more analytical in my thinking. She says that if I'd pay more attention to the way the detectives in her books think, I'd do better in school.

"You mean like a case?" she said.

I nodded.

"That's great, Sherm. A chance for you to exercise some logic. What's going on?"

I cleared my throat.

"You know Dini Trioli?"

Vanessa's eyebrows, which are nicely shaped,

went up again. "Yeah. That artist girl you've been crushing on."

"I'm not crushing on her. I just think she's . . . nice. Anyway, she's going out with Lester Broadside now."

"He's that guy with the good hair and the cool car, right?"

"Never mind all that."

"Sorry."

"I want to stay on topic here."

"Okay, so he's dating this girl. So?"

"So the thing is that I heard him talking to his buddies. I think Dini might be in danger."

That got her attention. Vanessa blinked slowly and focused her huge brown eyes on me. Her eyes are the drowning kind.

"What kind of danger?"

"Rick thinks—I mean, *I* think—Lester might be a Defiler."

Vanessa pursed her lips. I won't even get into how great it looked when she did that.

"Why do you think that?"

"The last girl he went out with got defiled. I heard him and his friends talking about it yesterday.

In the locker room."

"He said he was a Defiler?"

"No. Not exactly. But someone mentioned the big D."

"So you're just guessing that he's a Defiler."

"Isn't that how investigations work? People make guesses and then they follow them up."

"No. You're supposed to have evidence. Or at least some kind of a crime."

"I thought I should try to protect Dini, you know, *before* something happens."

Vanessa made a little lemon-tasting face that was gone almost as soon as I saw it.

"Sherm, if you want to investigate something worthwhile, why don't you investigate why people get defiled in this school and no one does anything about it?"

"Yeah, but isn't that a little . . ." What I wanted to say was, *Isn't that a little risky?* or *In case you haven't noticed, I'm just trying to go about my business.* But none of those sounded right, so I kept quiet.

"If you start looking into the defilings, you'll find out whether Lester's involved. If Dini's in danger, you'll save her. Most important, you'll be fixing something that needs to be fixed."

"People have been getting defiled here for a long time."

"So? Every girl here is afraid she'll get defiled. It's not right."

When she put it like that, her plan not only made sense, it sounded righteous. That's the thing about Vanessa: She always sounds like she's on the side of truth and justice.

"Okay," I said. "Maybe I'll take a look at it." I was feeling a little sick. Basically, Vanessa had just suggested that I take on the whole rotten system!

"This is great, Sherm. You're always saying how you might like to be a detective. This will be your first case."

The truth is, I'd never been serious when I said that. I was just trying to impress her. I'm actually not that interested in other people's business. What I'm interested in is girls.

"Don't worry," she said. "You won't be on your own in this. You've got me."

We were interrupted by a yell. It was Rick.

"I think this bitch is starting to burn!" he said, his voice as high and tight as a rusty hinge.

"And you've got Rick," added Vanessa.

"Sherman!" came Rick's voice from our side again. "It's burning!"

"Don't you feel confident now?" asked Vanessa.

I looked down at her pan. Brown smoke was rising out of it.

"Sherm!" cried Rick.

"Back off!" I said, because I could only deal with one burning omelet at a time, and a girl omelet was always going to get more attention from me than a boy omelet.

Vanessa was holding her spatula like a tennis racket. I watch a fair bit of Food Network television, so I could tell that her spatula-holding technique was strictly amateur hour.

"May I?" I asked, stepping in and taking it from her hand.

"Are you going to ruin our omelet?" asked Vanessa, sounding like she didn't much care one way or another.

I didn't ruin it. In one slick move I flipped it

and then stood back to let her and Edna admire, although Edna was too busy working her BlackBerry to notice.

"Nice work," said Vanessa. She sounded impressed, and right then I knew I could handle the Defilers and anything else that came my way.

Rick showed up at the entryway to Vanessa's kitchen cubicle. He was pale and his face was shiny with sweat.

"Sherm. I tried to turn it for you and everything fell out. On the stove," he said. "It's like the Hiroshima of omelets over there. It's nuked, man. And I didn't bring anything for lunch! You promised I'd get to eat in this class. I can't afford to have low blood sugar next period. I have a quiz!"

This explained the burned smell and stream of black smoke coming from the direction of our stove. Omelets may be the most stressful meal.

DEARLY DEFILED

Of all the mysteries in the world, why did defiling have to be the one I got sucked into investigating for my first case? It's like trying to find out why the sun comes up every day. Whatever happened to looking into problems with who's ripping off the chocolate bar dispenser in the vending machine—you know, Hardy Boys stuff?

The problem with defiling is that it's so secretive. No one is supposed to talk to the Defiled and no one does. If you do, you might end up defiled yourself.

I can't get defiled because, as far as I know, all the Defileds are girls. But how much would it suck if I was the first guy! That'd be something for the yearbook. "Sherman Mack: the first dude ever defiled at Harewood Technical School."

I'm not ready for this.

Thinking about my first case got me quite depressed, which my mother noticed as soon as I walked in the door. She may be abnormally youthful and obsessed with an inappropriate hobby, but you could never say she doesn't care about me. Other than her bad taste in names, clothing, dance style, and home décor, my mother is basically a good person.

That's something my grandparents seem to doubt. The problem is that my mother and my grandparents don't have a lot in common. My mom is a young, single-mother, burlesque-dancing bartender who works at the Blackberry Bush Pub in Nanaimo. My grandparents are permanently tanned retired people from West Vancouver who drive matching champagne-colored Lexuses and dress in pastel golf clothes and take a lot of vacations.

Even though my grandparents set my mother's teeth on edge, I like them and appreciate the huge fruit baskets with bottles of supplements and vitamins hidden underneath that they bring us every time they visit. I take about six pills a day to make up for the deficiencies in my diet. I'm pretty sure those vitamins are the only reason I've grown at all. Without the vitamins I'd probably have rickets and have topped out at three feet. Also, I think my grandparents help support us financially. My mom works hard at the pub, but there's no way she could afford me, her dancing costumes, and her wild lifestyle on her wages and tips.

I don't tell my mom that I know this and I take my vitamins in private so she doesn't feel inadequate.

"They think I don't feed you properly," she grumbled today as she picked bottles of B and C vitamins out from under the grapes and oranges in the latest basket. "It's offensive."

"Grandma and Grandpa came by today?"

"They were on their way to Qualicum to play golf with some of the other millionaires."

She took the new vitamin bottles over to the bathroom cupboard to join the others. Then she came back to her dinner of coffee and burned, unbuttered toast. My grandparents are right to be concerned about our eating habits.

"What's up, Sherm?" she asked. "You look sort of bummed."

"I'm okay."

"Come sit down," she said, and cleared a big heap of red feathers to one side of the table. "Sorry, I'm working on a new costume."

I sat.

"So what's going on?" she asked.

"Nothing."

"Really? Because you've got that look you get sometimes."

"What look?"

"The intense one. Like your head is about to explode."

"I'm fine."

"Are you sure? Is everything okay at school?"

"Yeah."

"No incidents?" Her voice had that slightly nervous tone to it, like she was a little afraid of what my answer would be.

I shook my head. I wished I could ask her if people got defiled when she was in high school but I didn't want her to worry. She worries quite a bit for such a young person. I sometimes think her dancing is her way of dealing with her nerves.

"So how's the second month of high school?" she asked.

"Fine. Okay."

"How's the love life? You dating anyone?"

"Mom," I said, because for God's sake.

"Okay. Just checking. You want some toast?"

"Sure."

"Oh, and I won't be here for dinner. I'm going to meet the girls for a practice before work. We're practicing some new routines. Adrienne just bought a pole. Lots of fun. Anyway, there's leftover pizza in the fridge."

I winced at the mention of the pole and prayed she wouldn't mention it in front of my friends. "Okay."

"Don't spend all night on the computer, either. Do homework or something."

She stood and brushed the crumbs off her skirt, which was not big and probably explains why she mostly eats toast.

"You're sure you're okay?"

"I'm fine."

"You know, honey, if you are having feelings for a girl all you need to do is show her the best part of yourself. You're a sensitive, brave young man. Let her know who you really are. Any girl with brains is going to see how great you are." Then she smiled at me, like we were sharing a secret. "Is it Vanessa?"

"Is what Vanessa?"

"Your crush."

I nearly fell out of my chair. "No. Vanessa's my friend. Jesus, Ma!"

"Don't say Jesus. Or Ma. This isn't the Ozarks. It would be okay if it was Vanessa. I like her. She's fierce. She'd make a great dancer."

She came over and kissed the top of my head. My brain was still caught on the idea of Vanessa in a burlesque outfit, and I barely heard the door close and the truck backfire about twelve times as my mom pulled out of the driveway.

Brave and sensitive. She might have something there. The question is, am I brave and sensitive enough to investigate defiling?

A LITTLE FRIENDLY

"Okay," said Rick the next morning. He was breathless from walking up the three stairs on our front porch. "I talked to my sister. She said Lester's last girlfriend, the one who got defiled, was named Farrah something and she was kind of sketchy."

He struggled to balance his huge stack of library books. He always carries them in front of him instead of in a backpack because he thinks it makes him look smarter and more masculine.

"She wondered why I was asking," he said.

Rick's sister Joan is in the twelfth grade. She has a New Wave hairstyle and is involved in backroom student politics.

"What did you tell her?" I asked.

"I told her I knew a girl who had the hots for him."

"And what did she say to that?"

"She laughed in my face and said something about any girl who knew me wouldn't be getting anywhere with Lester Broadside. I don't know what she meant by that."

I knew. She meant any girl who was friends with Rick probably wouldn't come out of the library long enough to catch Lester's eye.

"Are you sure this is a good idea?" he said. "You know, getting involved? Asking questions?"

"It's no big thing. I'm doing it for Dini. You know, finding out what she might be getting herself into with Lester."

"You're looking into defiling because Vanessa told you to."

"That's not true. It was on my list of things to do this year. Anyway, what does that mean, 'his last girlfriend was sketchy'?"

"My sister said the girl's whole scene was sort of low rent. You know, her family and stuff. Even before she got defiled."

"So why'd Lester go out with her? I thought he only dated Trophy Wives."

"Trophy Wives" is what the hottest girls in our school are called. They gather in front of the school in this area known as Trophy Wife Territory and wait for their boyfriends to pick them up. The Territory is Harewood's red carpet and VIP area all rolled into one. Everyone who is not a Trophy has to stand outside the velvet ropes.

"Dini's not a Trophy," Rick pointed out.

"What's that supposed to mean, jackass?"

"Turn down the touchy dial. I'm just saying . . . Dini's cool but she's independent. She doesn't run in the usual circles."

"Hmmff."

"Dude, you need someone on the dark side to hook you up."

He was right. I needed an informant. Someone who knew their way around the seedy side of life, because that's where I was headed if I was going to start talking to defiled people.

I knew just the person.

★ ★ ★

As soon as we got to school, I told Rick I had something to do and left him to wait for the library to open. I walked over to the far wing, to the boys' washroom hardly anybody uses, also known as the Can Too Far or the C.T.F. It's where Ed the Head works.

Ed's the main connection for pot smokers in the school. The only people who don't seem clued into this are the teachers.

Ed's also supposed to be the one person who knows everything and everyone. I met him on my third day, when I got two detentions in a row for showing up late to class because I stayed up most of the night on the computer, which is something that happens when your mom is a bartender and you don't have enough supervision.

I looked around the hallway to make sure no teachers would see me going into the C.T.F. My stomach was upset. I had only just started my investigation, and I thought I might be getting an ulcer.

The C.T.F. only had two stalls and there was someone in the far one.

I cleared my throat. "Ah, Ed?"

I could see a pair of huge, white Nike running shoes under the door.

"Ed's not here." The voice was high pitched, like someone trying to disguise his voice.

"It's just me. Sherman. Sherman Mack."

The shoes disappeared off the floor.

"Ed. It's Sherman Mack. We had detention together a couple of times. First week of school."

Nothing. I'd hoped I wouldn't have to do this.

"You liked my mom," I said.

The shoes hit the floor.

"You the kid with the foxy mama?"

I winced. The worst thing about Ed the Head wasn't the drug dealing. It was the way he checked out my mom when she came to pick me up from detention. Ed the Head took one look at my mom in her dance leotard and never got over it.

I considered leaving. I didn't want to hear all of Ed's sick fantasies about asking out my mother. Just between you and me, guys with older moms who dress properly have no idea how lucky they are. Seriously.

"Your mom's the one who wears those little black tights with the little short skirt, man? She's got that—"

"Yeah, yeah," I said quickly, cutting him off before he could say anything else.

The runners shuffled around and the bathroom door opened a crack.

A bloodshot brown eye peered out of the opening.

"Little dude. You here because your moms wants to go on that date?"

I fought back the urge to punch him. If it was anyone else, I'd have lost it already. But Ed the Head is even smaller than me. Shorter, lighter. He's all hair and runners. His drug stash is probably the only thing about him that has any weight.

His eye flicked past me to the bathroom door.

"There's no one else here," I said.

He stepped out of the toilet stall.

Ed the Head is like a movie director's idea of a teenage dealer. He has the wild head of brown curly hair, the white high-tops, the Judas Priest T-shirt, and the plaid shirt over top. He isn't a bad-looking guy. I heard that before he stopped growing, lots of girls wanted a piece of his action. Now he gets them because of his line of work.

"So, you in the market for a little friendly?" he asked. *Friendly* is Ed's word for pot. He takes a lot of pride in making up new terminology. English teachers don't give young people in the drug subculture enough credit for being creative.

"No, thanks. I have a question for you."

"You want to know what your curfew's going to be when I become your step old man?" His laugh was a raspy cackle.

"Ha," I said.

"Seriously, dude. Your moms, she's—"

"Yeah. I got it. I was wondering if you could help me find someone."

"Hey, man! I haven't seen you in detention lately."

"I've been keeping out of trouble. Getting to school on time. All that."

"How you staying mellow? You scoring off someone else?" He looked hurt at the thought I might be buying drugs from someone else. For some reason, Ed's convinced that I'm some huge drug addict. I have no idea why. Maybe he assumes all us shorter guys are.

"No. I'm just keeping a low profile," I said.

"You're maturing. Sweet. Still, you should come back to detention. I had a good time buggin' on you."

"Thanks."

"And if you need a little herbal remedy to chill, you come to me. I'll hook you up."

"Thanks. As soon as I'm ready to . . . do that, you'll be my first stop. But like I was saying, I was wondering if you knew where I could find someone."

"They like the friendly?" he asked. "They like the love?"

I assumed *love* was related to *friendly*. Maybe it was a bit stronger. "Probably. I'm looking for a girl. I wondered if you might know her. Her name's Farrah."

His face closed. All at once I was looking at Ed, angry drug dealer dude, not Ed the Head, dealer of love and friendliness.

"You're not supposed to consort with her.

She's D-listed, man," he said.

"I was just wondering—"

"The D-listed have enough troubles." He didn't look so small anymore.

"I just wanted to ask her a few questions."

"You trying to set me up?" He looked around, like there might be a wiretap in one of the toilet stalls. I wondered for a second if he was going to attack me.

"Are you trying to prove that I treat with the Defiled? You trying to get my ass in a sling?"

Treat with the Defiled? I began to suspect Ed was getting high on his own supply.

"No. I just wanted to know . . . what happened."

"She got defiled, fool. What else you need to know?"

"I want to know why. What happened?"

He glanced sideways at the door. It was getting late. Pretty soon his other customers would start showing up.

"They say you know everyone and everything in this school."

He looked a little calmer at that.

"You don't know jack."

"Not personally, no."

Ed made a disgusted noise and said, "Grade nines." As though that explained everything.

"It's not really about Farrah," I said. "It's about my friend. I think she might be next. She just started going out with Lester Broadside."

Ed's lips were pressed tight together. He brushed back his big curly hair. "Prick."

"Who? Do you mean Lester?"

Something moved in his face, but he didn't answer.

"So you know Farrah?" I asked.

"She's my second cousin. She's real nice, too. At least she was. Before they put her on the list. Her life was no trip to Boston Pizza before that, either. Her mom's kind of messed up. Her old man's a piece of shit. But Farrah was okay, you know. Pricks."

I gulped. "Do you know who the Defilers are?"

"I got my suspicions."

"Do you know where I can find Farrah?"

"Who's this friend of yours? The one you're so worried about?"

For some reason I didn't want to say Dini's name out loud.

"It's just this girl I know."

Ed stared hard at me from under his mop of hair.

"Broadside's a doucheweed. So are his friends. You want to talk to Farrah, look for her at the Fun Centre. She'll probably be there with whoever she's going out with right now. I don't think she comes around school much anymore. She's supposed to be taking classes at the Alternate but I haven't seen her there."

"Thanks, Ed."

The bell rang outside, echoing down the hall.

"I need a smoke," he said. He looked at me and lifted his chin. "You know, I told Farrah to stay away from Broadside. I said he was just messing with her. It was a game with him and his shittard friends. I told her that guys like him didn't go out with girls like her. But she wouldn't listen. She thought he was in love or some shit."

I nodded.

"This school blows. When a guy can't even be

seen talking to his own second cousin."

"I know," I said.

Ed sighed and turned back into Mr. Stoner Guy.

"Good luck, man. And hey! Tell your moms that offer to take her to dinner at the DQ is good anytime. They got a bottomless Coke there. I'll treat her right."

"Thanks," I said, and walked out the door as two punk rock guys pushed their way into the bathroom.

8

FARRAH FAWCETT
DOESN'T LIVE HERE ANYMORE

After school Vanessa and Rick and I walked over to the tennis courts at Bowen Park to meet our friend Ashton for a game. It felt more like July than October, but the light was strange, like someone put a dirty filter over the sun. Although we aren't jocks, we enjoy a game of tennis now and then. There are lots of free courts around town and most of the people who play at them aren't that good, which is nice. Some of them even smoke between sets, which you don't see every day.

We met Ashton at the tennis courts a few years ago and he told us some interesting and little-known facts about sex and we've been friends ever since. He and his younger brother Bennett are tutored at home because their parents couldn't find a fancy enough private school around here. If I was the type to get jealous, Ashton's someone I'd be jealous of. He's rich and tall and even though I know I'm not supposed to notice, he's good-looking. He can draw and paint, and he's like this total master on the subject of sex. Seriously. His parents even let him study it, like as one of his school subjects. Ashton is probably the most mature fifteen-year-old in the world.

When we got to Bowen, Ashton and Bennett were waiting with their rackets. They were dressed all in white: white shorts, white T-shirts, and white visors. Ashton mixed it up a bit with some checkerboard Vans, which looked wicked cool.

"Gentlemen, what's happening?" said Ashton.

Bennett didn't say anything. He's not much of a talker. He doesn't play tennis, either. He just sits on the bench and stares into space. Ashton says he's thinking about physics, but I bet he's thinking about sex. Either that or he's autistic. Apparently a lot of very smart people are autistic, but that doesn't automatically mean they can play the piano. That's a misconception from the movie *Rain Man*, in which Dustin Hoffman plays an autistic person.

"You'll be happy to hear that Sherman is finally going to do something useful with his life," said Vanessa.

Ashton cocked his head to the side as we headed for the lower court, far away from the other players. Rick's shots have a tendency to go wild and hit parked cars.

"Sherm is taking on the whole rotten system," said Rick. "In other words, he's a dead man. This may be the last time you see him."

"No, I'm not. I'm just looking into this thing at our school. I'm going to talk to this girl."

"What girl?" asked Ashton.

I felt paranoid talking about it in public. What if someone was hiding behind the practice wall and overheard? You can't go around telling everyone that you're going to talk to a defiled person.

"Just this girl."

"One of the Defiled," said Rick, in a drama-club whisper.

"Come again?" said Ashton.

lot. My first thought was that the Fun Centre didn't look very fun. It's a square, cement building that sits in the middle of a parking lot like someone dropped it there by accident. All the windows are blacked out.

I'd been watching the place for half an hour, trying to keep a low profile, but it was tough, because the parking lot was empty and no one ever seemed to come in or out. The place had very shitty Fun Shui or whatever you call that Chinese energy.

I'd never been in the Opposite-of-Fun Centre before. I just always assumed it was a front for some kind of criminal activity. It's possible that I'm developing one of those naturally suspicious minds that cops and private investigators get from dealing with the criminal element all the time.

My butt was getting sore from sitting on the concrete divider. I couldn't take waiting anymore. If the defiled girl, Farrah Savoie, was in there, I was wasting precious time. I walked over, pushed open the door, and stepped inside.

The Fun Centre was just as dark inside as it looked from the outside. A guy sat on a high stool behind a counter to my right. There was a single small spotlight trained on his comic book. Beyond him I could see rows of video terminals with people huddled around them. Beeps, pings, and the sound of car crashes and gunfire rose up into a wall of electronic noise. The place smelled like electromagnetic static and chip bags and unwashed hair.

"Help you?" asked the guy behind the counter.

"I'm just looking for someone." I might as well have mouthed the words, for all the chance there was of him hearing me.

He went back to reading his comic.

I walked down a row of games. No one turned around to look at me. At the end of the center aisle a thin sliver of light shone through a crack at the bottom of a door that was painted the same flat black as the walls.

I looked around to see if anyone was watching. No one was. I turned the doorknob and walked in.

The room beyond was long and skinny, as bright as the gaming room was dark. There were two pool tables laid out lengthwise on one side and two round tables on the other side.

A man, maybe in his late twenties or early thirties, was playing pool with a girl who was maybe a few years older than me. She was about as wide as her pool cue and her hair looked like the before example in a before-and-after extra body shampoo commercial. Still, she was reasonably attractive.

Guys in construction boots and heavy canvas jackets were playing poker at one of the round tables. No one paid any attention to me, so I said "Excuse me," and faded back into the darkness of the arcade again.

Now that I'd seen all of it, the Fun Centre still didn't seem fun. I decided to wait outside.

It took a second for my eyes to adjust to daylight and I went back to my spot on the concrete divider across from the front door. Why would any girl, even a defiled one, want to hang out someplace so depressing? I thought only guys went to places like that. I spent a few minutes being bored and wondering if it was too soon to leave. I decided to give it five more minutes.

To help pass the time, I tried meditating. Our

health teacher says deep breathing can help with the stress of being an adolescent, but in my experience it just makes me think about girls.

I'd been meditating for the better part of a minute when a car pulled into the Fun Centre parking lot—an older brown Buick sedan. Total jalopy.

The driver, who was tall and had a full-on mullet and sideburns, got out of the car and walked around to the passenger side. He had on new cowboy boots, the kind people only wear in town. He opened the door and a girl stepped out. Somehow, I knew it was Farrah. She was better looking than I expected, but she looked tired and way, way older than me, even though she was only supposed to be sixteen or maybe seventeen, tops. I couldn't stop staring. I'd never seen a defiled person up close before.

I hadn't expected Farrah to be so . . . I don't want to say hot because she's defiled and defiled people can't really be hot, but she was definitely interesting. She was very thin and tallish, like 5' 7" or 5' 8". Her shoulders were slumped, the way you see sometimes on tall girls. She had on jeans and a jean jacket. Both were kind of faded. In fact, everything about her was a little faded, even her skin. It was like being defiled had washed her out. She reminded me of one of those small brown birds that blends into its environment, the kind where if you watch it long enough you start to see that it's kind of amazing.

I got up and walked toward them.

At first they didn't notice me. The mullet guy was saying something and Farrah was staring at her feet.

"Okay?" I heard the guy say. I coughed to let them know I was there. They turned.

"Excuse me," I said.

"Yeah?" said the guy.

Farrah's long, light brown hair hung in her pale face.

"Are you Farrah?" I asked.

As soon as I spoke, the guy's face closed, the same way Ed the Head's had.

"I wanted to ask her, to ask you, I mean," I said, looking from the guy to Farrah, "a couple of questions about something at school."

71

"She don't go to school no more," said the guy.

"I do sometimes," she said so softly I could barely hear her. "I go to the Alternate. Part-time."

"What do you want to ask her?" asked the guy. He had a harsh case of the hostiles. I got ready to run in case he came after me.

It occurred to me that for a defiled person, Farrah had a lot of guys looking out for her.

"Dan," she said. "He's just a kid."

"I thought none of the little shits from that school talk to you anymore," he said to her.

She bit her bottom lip and stared down at her feet again.

"Fine. You want to talk to him, go ahead. I'll be in the back room playing hold 'em with Tony. You come right in when you're done." He shot me a look that was all the warning I needed, and walked away. Stones crunched under the hard heels of his boots.

"What do you want?" Farrah asked when we were alone.

"I've got a few questions."

I forced myself not to look over my shoulder. I

was talking to a Defiled in broad daylight!

Farrah pulled her hair back with both hands like she was opening a pair of curtains and I could see that with a little color in her cheeks and a smile, she'd be something.

"Look, little man," she said. "You're going to get in trouble if anyone sees you talking to me."

"My name is Mack," I said. "Sherman Mack. I'm a couple of years behind you in school. I just started ninth grade."

"Little man, we don't even go to school in the same universe."

I'd hoped that telling her my name would get her to stop calling me "little man." No luck.

"Yeah, well, about that," I said.

She looked away, half bored, half worried. She hitched her long purse strap up her thin shoulder.

I was having trouble bringing up her defiled-ness. Do the Defiled know they're defiled? The fact that no one talks to them makes it hard to talk to them.

"So that guy who dropped you off, is he your . . . ?"

"My what?" Her voice was defensive.

I had a powerful urge to give up my career as a P.I.

"I was just wondering if he was your boyfriend."

If I could have kicked my own ass right then, I would have. Why did I ask that? It wasn't my business. Why hadn't I read something about conducting interviews before trying to do one? I should have paid more attention to Vanessa's crime books. I usually just skimmed them to get to the sexy or violent parts.

"Why would *you* want to know that?"

Most of the women the detectives interview in Vanessa's books want to sleep with the detectives as soon as they see them. Looked like I wasn't going to have that problem.

"Nothing. I mean, no reason. Your cousin, Ed the . . . Ed said I'd be able to find you here. He said that you hung out here with your boyfriends."

She wrinkled her nose, which was small and straight, and yanked on her purse strap again. The purse was decorated with a rhinestone bird. Quite a few of the stones had fallen off, leaving the outline incomplete.

"Dan's my older brother. He's here making sure I don't get a boyfriend."

"Oh, that's good," I said.

"Excuse me?"

"No, I mean, it's nice that your brother cares."

"Whatever. I can look after myself. Why did you want to talk to me?" she said. "I don't have time to stand around here all day."

Like she had somewhere really important to be.

"You want to talk inside?" I asked, trying to give the impression I would do it as a favor to her and not because I was scared to be seen with her.

She gave me a "screw you" look, then said, "No, out here is fine."

"Right. I was wondering about last year, about what happened. Do you know why you . . ."

I couldn't figure out how to complete that sentence.

She jerked up the purse strap again.

I decided to lay it on the line.

"I've got this friend. She's going out with Lester Broadside, just like you did. I'm worried that she's going to get, you know. Like you."

Farrah winced a little when I said Lester's name. When I stopped speaking, she dragged a hand through her long hair. Her eyes had gone from mad to sad.

"Defiled," she said.

I nodded. "I was hoping you'd tell me what you know. About what happened."

"I know it's like being murdered, only you're still walking around."

"So what happened? Who put you on the list?"

She shrugged. Her purse strap had fallen down her arm again but this time she didn't seem to notice. It dangled from the crook of her elbow.

"You went out with Lester Broadside. Was it him?"

A wave of hurt passed across her face and I wished I hadn't asked the question.

"There are a few of us who've been defiled at school. I'm the only one who went out with Lester."

She sounded sadder than anything.

"But could it have been him?"

"Who cares who it was?" she said.

All her brown-bird prettiness was gone. She looked ruined.

"So what if someone put my picture on a few bathroom mirrors," she said. "It takes the rest of you losers to defile someone."

I stepped back as her words hit me.

"Me?"

"As far as I'm concerned, every single person in that school is a Defiler," she said.

"But I just started at Harewood."

"You know who Farrah Fawcett was? She was this blond chick, a big deal back in the seventies. She was in some movies and she had this famous poster where she was wearing a bathing suit. When I was born, my mom thought I was going to be so pretty and popular. Just like Farrah Fawcett. Instead I got treated like crap all the way through grade school. Last year I made some changes. I started feeling better, more confident. Looking better. Lester noticed me. Asked me out. He was so nice to me. I was having my Farrah moment, you know? Just like my mom always thought I would. Then somebody posted my picture in the bathrooms and the rest of you practically fell all over yourselves to ruin my life. Now my mom makes my thirty-year-old brother go everywhere with me because she's worried I'm going to do something to myself. And the real Farrah Fawcett has cancer in her private area. Anyway, I'm sick of talking about this," she said.

She really did sound sick of it.

"I'm sorry." I couldn't think of anything else to say.

"Look, I'll give you the names of a couple of other girls. There are more, but they've all dropped out. Maybe one of them will know more than I do."

"You don't talk to each other?" I asked.

She laughed, a low sound. "It's crazy, isn't it? Even we don't want to talk to each other."

She dug around in her purse and pulled out a crumpled slip of paper and a pen and scribbled a few words.

"If your friend does get D-listed, she'll find out what Lester's made of. You'll find out what you're made of, too," she said. Then she handed me the piece of paper, hitched up her long purse strap once more, and headed for the front door of the Fun Centre. She was halfway across the parking lot when I called after her.

"Farrah?"

She turned.

"I'm sorry," I said again.

She stared right at me, not smiling, not frowning.

Then she disappeared into the black glass doors of the Fun Centre.

As I walked out of the parking lot, I noticed a black Honda Civic with tinted windows pull out across the street and drive slowly away. I couldn't see who was inside.

THE OPERATION

When I got home after talking to Farrah, my mom had already left for work. I sat at the kitchen table, which was covered in magazines and old toast plates. I pulled out the piece of paper Farrah had given me, a bank slip that showed a balance of $5.17. I didn't recognize the names she'd written down, but that didn't mean much.

I thought about Farrah saying that if Dini gets defiled she's going to find out what Lester's made of and that I'll find out what I'm made of. I'm pretty sure I'm made of good stuff. My mom is. My grandparents are. But who knows about my father. For all I know, he might be made of the cheapest, most jalopy stuff in the world.

I couldn't stand the thought of Dini ending up like Farrah, half destroyed by some pointless social conspiracy. It wasn't going to be enough to investigate defiling. I had to show Dini that I'm a man of substance, preferably get her away from potential danger *before* she ended up on a bathroom mirror. Maybe she wasn't in danger. But even if she wasn't, I was going to show Dini who I was.

I smoothed and folded the bank statement and put it back in my pocket. I'd decide what to do about the other defiled girls later. Then I reached for the phone. This plan was going to require teamwork.

When the bell rang the next day at 3:15 I was already in position near Trophy Wife Territory.

Standing right by the Territory was a bit emasculating, but also sort of exciting. I felt like one of those guys who take pictures of celebrities going into movie premieres.

I squeezed my eyes shut for a second and tried to tell myself that my team was in place and ready for action. When I looked up it seemed like girls were coming out of every doorway.

Then the Trophies walked out the front doors and everything else seemed to fade away. They were like a *Girls Gone Wild* video come to life. Long hair swinging, they cleared less hot girls out of their way like tigers walking through a petting zoo. The light seemed to change around them and get brighter.

In the lead was Vargo. She's in eleventh grade and one of those highly complex and attractive girls with a lot of personal issues that she's extremely open about, such as eating disorders and depression and cutting herself. It's almost like she's trying out the problems. She's an excellent public speaker and a spokesperson for all the girls. Whenever a camera crew comes to school to get the youth perspective, they end up talking to Vargo.

It helps that she's as close to perfect-looking as a girl can get. Vargo has the bee-stung lip thing going on, as well as shiny black hair and some other things I won't get into.

She goes out with Pete March, who is the editor of the school newspaper. Rick and I went to a couple of journalism club meetings in our first week at Harewood, not because we want to be reporters but because we knew Pete ran the meetings and we hoped Vargo might stop by. She didn't, so we stopped going. Still, she gave a talk at our first assembly so I feel like I know quite a bit about her, including what she thinks of global warming (she's against it), globalization (against it), feminism (for it), Wicca (for it), and premarital sex (for it). She has also experienced depression, but doesn't take medication because she doesn't want to become part of the pharmaceutical industrial complex.

She basically floats my boat. Big time.

To Vargo's left was Clarissa Kim, a rock-climbing, river-rafting, eleventh-grade pothead who usually wears her hair in braids. She carried a helmet decorated with surfer stickers that she probably got from actually surfing, unlike 90 percent of other people who have surf stickers plastered everywhere. Clarissa has a great raspy laugh. She goes out with Randy Leland, a welder and motocross champion who graduated at least a couple of years ago.

I don't mean to sound critical, but I'm not sure Randy is worthy of her. I mean, what does he have that I don't? You know, besides a soul patch, sideburns, motorcycle, a good job, and, if the rumors are true, a steady connection to high-grade marijuana?

Raquel George was on Vargo's right. She is three kinds of hot with a side of extra smoking hot. She has long blond hair, is the president of the debating club, gets the highest grades in the whole school, and dates Tal Manhas, who is rich and a top lacrosse player. Lacrosse is the biggest sport at Harewood, probably because it's so violent. Tal Manhas looks like a model in one of those men's cologne ads, except for a lacrosse scar on his face.

Other girls hang out in Trophy Wife Territory, but Vargo, Clarissa, and Raquel are the crème de la crème, the top prizes, if you want to think of it that way. Ask any guy in this school who he dreams about at night and I bet it would be one of these three girls.

As the girls came closer, I started to get an intense flight-or-fight feeling. The girls didn't even seem to notice me. They're used to being stared at. If one of them had looked my way I would have stroked out.

I prayed that I was right and Dini would be getting picked up from the Territory now that she was dating Lester. A second later, Dini answered my prayer when she came out the front door and headed straight for the Territory. She fit in perfectly. She had on a plain white shirt with some embroidery on it and short pants and ballet flats. If she'd been in a bathing suit or a strapless gown she couldn't have looked better.

"Hi, Dini!" I said, maybe a little too loud.

She looked around and smiled, confused to see me standing near all of Harewood's turbo hotties.

"Oh, hi, Sherm. How are you?"

"Whatcha doing?" I asked, ignoring her question.

"I'm meeting someone."

At that moment Lester's car started up in the parking lot. I knew it was his because his sounds like a jet engine getting ready for takeoff.

It was time. I gave the signal by pretending to yawn and pumping my fists into the air a couple of times, the way a person does when he's yawning.

The move took Dini by surprise. She stepped back and said, "Whoa. Watch the flying fists, okay?"

We'll see who watches what, I thought to myself.

Clarissa Kim jumped on the back of Randy

Leland's KLR 650, and they burned away. Then Pete pulled up on his scooter, Vargo threw her leg over the back, and they were gone. Raquel slid into Tal Manhas's Prelude. Then there were just a few assorted hotties, me, and Dini.

I yawned and stretched again, giving the final signal. The big red double doors to the woodworking shop flew open and Ashton staggered out, Rick right behind him. I picked Ashton to play the injured guy because he's homeschooled so Dini won't know him.

Ashton held his arm like a favorite pet that got hit by a car. Hit hard. Blood leaked everywhere. It dripped onto the pavement. In fact, blood was pretty much *pouring* onto the pavement. My vision went a little blurry, even though I knew the blood wasn't real.

Rick looked around like he needed help. He was overacting, like Paris Hilton in a porn video, but I was too dizzy to signal for him to tone it down.

"Help," yelled Rick. "Help!"

I tried to move but couldn't. My motor skills were gone. Everything froze. This was bad news because my entire plan was built around two sure things:

1. Lester the Molester would never risk ruining his clothes by coming to the rescue of a wounded-in-shop-class stranger. (I doubt Lester would help a *family member*.)
2. If I did help, I'd look like a hero.

I finally convinced one of my legs to move and the other to follow it. I tried to run over to help Ashton in a way that was both courageous and sensitive, but I seemed to have a major case of the wobblies. I'd only staggered a couple of steps toward him when Dini pushed me out of the way and elbowed Rick out of her way, like a linebacker heading for a touchdown. She dropped her black sketchbook and started grabbing at Ashton's arm, trying to get a look at his injured hand. He pulled it away from her, trying to hide his fake injury.

This wasn't how it was supposed to go down! The plan was for me to show leadership as I courageously led Ashton into the washroom. Dini and the rest of the Trophy Wives were going to stare after me with admiration and a touch of light lust. Rick was going to stay near Dini and say things like, "Man, I had no idea what to do there. Thank God Sherm was here."

And after it was all over, Dini was supposed to look at Lester and the scales would fall from her eyes and she'd see that even though he has a sweet ride and good hair, he hasn't got much in the way of real guts. I would be the hero.

Unfortunately, my plan didn't count on Dini being some kind of a first-aid prodigy. Also, it seems like I might not be too good with blood.

Lester had pulled over in front of the Territory but showed no signs of getting out. I was so dizzy I could barely see, but I think I saw him cleaning his nails while Dini went after Ashton with her mad aggressive first-aid skills.

Rick stood off to the side, saying, "Oh, man. Oh, man," while Dini tried to force Ashton to show her his injured arm.

"Let go," Dini told Ashton in a fierce voice. "Let me look!"

I had to get over there and take charge, but my feet wouldn't move. A second later, everything went black.

When I woke up Dini was staring into my eyes. I smiled, to let her know I was okay. To show her what I was made of.

"Freak," she said. Then she gave me a little nudge with her foot. I suppose the technical term for it would be a kick.

"But—"

"I can't believe you," she said. There were red stains all over her pretty white blouse. Then she disappeared. I heard a car door open and close. Lying there on the sidewalk, I could actually feel the sidewalk vibrate as the car pulled away. I closed my eyes. When I opened them again Ashton and Rick stood over me. Ashton had blood all over his white sweater and pants. He looked like a mass-murdering tennis player.

"The operation was not a success," he said.

I closed my eyes and left them that way.

THE BIG D

On Monday it seemed like almost everybody had heard about the fake-accident incident. A few people called me "Blood Boy." Not one person seemed to think there was anything very sensitive or courageous about fainting at the sight of fake blood and then getting kicked by the girl of your dreams.

After getting razzed all morning, I was relieved to get to cooking class. Now I know why it's so common for private investigators to have hobbies and things they do to unwind, such as fishing and building very small boats in bottles. Detecting is exhausting work. I looked forward to making something nice to eat and talking to Vanessa about what happened.

But first Mrs. Samuels had a big announcement.

She made us gather around the prep table with the big mirror angled over top so we could learn the proper knife technique for julienning carrots or the correct wrist action for beating egg whites. The mirror is also handy for getting a top-down perspective on some of the girls.

"Everyone! Everyone!" said Mrs. Samuels as we stood around, tying our apron strings.

"I have very exciting news!"

Mrs. Samuels thinks everything is exciting. If the cookies come out perfect, that's exciting. If someone pulls off al dente pasta she practically goes hysterical with joy. She's a pretty good teacher. After all, too much enthusiasm is way better than none. Also, she has this very nice giggle. She's not too young or anything, but she giggles like she's about six years old when she gets really excited. I like her.

"As you know, Cooking Nine and Cooking Ten are the prerequisites to get into the Cafeteria Program."

Eleventh and twelfth graders in the Cafeteria Program make all the lunches for the whole school and even put on a special brunch for the teachers on

Fridays. They get to miss a lot of regular classes and from what I heard, you were pretty much guaranteed a restaurant job if you finished school with two years of Cafeteria under your belt. I was seriously considering it. You know, unless Harvard tries to recruit me for one of their sports-avoidance teams.

"This year we've decided that a few special Cooking Nines who distinguish themselves may have the opportunity to be fast-tracked into the Cafeteria Program."

No one said anything. Finally, I put up my hand. "What does that mean, exactly?"

"Good question, Sherman!" said Mrs. Samuels. "It means we are implementing a special project for the Cooking Nines! You will be the first group of ninth graders at Harewood Technical to get the opportunity to work in a professional kitchen starting in tenth grade!"

Mrs. Samuels was beginning to hyperventilate a little. Her eyes were bugging out. I could see them protruding in the overhead mirror.

"So what's this special project?" said Rick. He

didn't sound nearly as excited as Mrs. Samuels.

"We've decided that those of you who are really, really keen on the culinary arts"—she stopped speaking and looked right at Rick—"people like you, Richard, will be allowed to undertake a final project that will enable you to go straight into Cafeteria next year."

She looked around, her face shining like she was about to reveal something amazing, like we were all secretly possessed of supernatural cooking powers and destined to cook in the Enchanted Garden.

"We are going to allow you to put on a dinner party!" she said with a huge smile.

We looked at each other.

"Do we have to?" asked Edna, Vanessa's depressing partner.

Mrs. Samuels frowned, but only for a second. "No, of course not. This opportunity is just for those very special, very keen students!"

"I barely even know what a dinner party is," said one guy.

"Where will we have it? Who will come?" asked another.

"What will we cook?" asked someone else.

"This is the great part! You will have to come up with a theme. It can be an ethnic theme or a more general theme."

"Like Christmas?" asked a girl. "Is Christmas considered a theme?"

"No, idiot. That's a holiday," said her partner.

"Christmas food could certainly be a theme. But you will be presenting your dinner at the end of the school year, so you'll want to keep that in mind. You will submit your menu to me for approval. Then you will put on your dinner party for your guests one evening here at school while I supervise. And at the end of the year, we will create a Cooking Nine Cookbook with all of your menus." Mrs. Samuels sighed and clasped her hands to her chest, like a squirrel with a nut. "It's going to be so much fun!"

"Oh, man," muttered one guy, sounding over-whelmed. "That's some crazy shit."

"It's optional, man. Don't have an episode," said his partner.

"And we can invite anyone to our dinner party?" I asked. "Not just people from the class?"

"That's right, Sherm!"

"Sign me up!" I was so excited I probably sounded like Mrs. Samuels.

As soon as Mrs. Samuels gave us our assignment for the class—macaroni and cheese, sweet!—and sent us back to our stations, I headed over to check in on Vanessa and Edna.

"Well, if it isn't Mr. Sign Me Up," said Edna, whose personality hadn't improved since last class.

I ignored her and looked at Vanessa. "You are coming to my dinner party, right? It's going to be wicked."

"Kind of like your little performance in front of the school yesterday?" she said.

"That was just a misunderstanding."

"What kind of misunderstanding?"

"I got Ashton to pretend to have an accident in the shop."

"Why?"

"So I could help him out."

"But instead you fainted?"

"There was a lot of blood," I said.

"Fake blood," added Rick, who'd followed me over, holding the block of cheddar and the cheese grater. "We used three bags. Probably should have used just one."

"And you did this why?"

"He was trying to show off for Dini," said Rick.

"Sherman, what were you thinking? You said you were going to investigate the defilings, not stalk Dini Trioli. One of these days she's going to—"

"Kick his ass? Too late," said Rick.

Vanessa wiped her hands on the front of her apron, which was a little bit tight on her. Something about the way her apron fit made my stomach, or a bit lower down, actually, feel funny.

"I wasn't stalking her. I was just showing her—"

"You were just making a jackass of yourself."

"I did other stuff, too." I lowered my voice. "I talked to one of them. One of the Defiled."

Vanessa's perfect eyebrows rose and I lost my train of thought, thinking about all of Vanessa's perfectly shaped parts.

"Hello? You were saying something?" she said, her eyebrows going even higher, until they were like McDonald's arches, only dark.

"Right. Sorry. The one I talked to didn't think Lester was . . . you know. And she told me the names of some of the other . . . ones."

"Ones?" asked Rick.

"Defiled people," I said.

Vanessa nodded. "Just when I think you're completely hopeless. So are you going to keep investigating?"

I nodded and she looked impressed.

"So she really kicked you?" said Vanessa.

"It was more of a light tap really."

"She booted his ass," said Rick.

Vanessa shook her head. "She didn't need to do that," she said, which made me feel warm all over.

Before we could talk any more we were interrupted by the teacher.

"Okay, people," said Mrs. Samuels. "Richard and Sherman, please take yourselves back to your own unit and get cooking. This homemade macaroni and cheese isn't going to make itself!"

Rick headed back to our kitchenette, and I followed. When I looked back at Vanessa she smiled, and my stomach flopped again.

I was so busy thinking about what her smile did to my insides that I smacked right into Rick, who'd stopped dead in front of me.

"What's that?" asked Rick.

A photograph lay on our counter.

"I don't know," I said.

He picked it up. "Dude, it's you."

I grabbed it from him. It took a half a minute for the image to register. It was a picture of me standing in a parking lot, talking to Farrah.

"Who's the chick?" asked Rick. Then something caught his eye.

"Sherm," he said.

I turned the picture around. In small block letters someone had drawn a box, and in the box was a D.

"What the hell does that mean?" asked Rick.

I couldn't answer. I was too busy trying to remember how to breathe.

I turned to Juan and Felipe, the cousins from El Salvador who share the station behind ours.

"Hey," I said, trying to control the shaking in

my voice. "Did you guys see anyone over here? I mean by our stuff?"

Felipe stroked his barely there mustache.

"No, man. We got hung up with the cheese sauce. Had to consult Mrs. S."

"Juan? Did you notice anyone at our station?"

Juan shook his head.

I walked over to the station across from us. Morgan and Bethany were leaning against their counter, eating pieces of cheese.

"Did either of you see anyone at our station?"

Morgan rolled her eyes at me. "Like I pay attention to what you do, Sherman Mack. Dream on."

I was reminded again why I decided to move on to older girls.

Bethany shook her head, which was covered in purple spikes. "I never see anything when there's cheese."

Rick came up behind me. "Did anyone see anything?" But I was already on my way to Vanessa and Edna's station.

"Did you see anyone over at our area when I was talking to you?"

Vanessa shook her head. Edna ignored me.

Then Mrs. Samuels appeared.

"Sherman Mack, I've watched you visiting all over this room when you should be cooking. If you're going to be one of my very, very keen final project people, you're going to need to learn to focus in the kitchen!"

She touched my shoulder to turn me around and nudged me back in the direction of our station.

"I feel like I've been rounding up students left and right this period. Some of them don't even take this class."

I turned to her.

"What do you mean? Rounding up what students?"

Mrs. Samuels paused to think. "Well, there was you and Richard. And Felipe. I had to send him back to his station. There was one boy who isn't even in this class. And now you again."

"You kicked out some guy who wasn't in our class? Who was he? Do you know his name? Was he hanging around our station?"

"Sherman, I'm not joking. You need to get

cooking or your pasta's not even going to hit the al dente mark!"

I resisted the urge to take her by the shoulders and shake her.

"The guy, Mrs. Samuels. I have to know who he was."

"I've never seen him before, Sherman. I've only been at the school since September."

I interrupted her. "Would you remember him if you saw him again?"

Mrs. Samuels seemed to remember that she was the teacher and not a suspect in a crime show.

"Enough questions, Sherman. Get to work."

I stumbled back to make macaroni and cheese.

FAIR WARNING

It's funny how a single photograph can change your whole life. Rick was gone when I got back to our cubicle. In a daze, I put on the water to boil. I was so distracted I burned the butter and forgot to add the flour to thicken the cheese sauce.

Someone had seen me talking to Farrah. I looked at the photo again. Was it a warning? Or a threat? The shot had been taken from the direction of the Fun Centre. Whoever took that picture had been inside! I tried to think. Had I seen anyone coming in or out? Had I recognized anyone I'd seen inside?

Then I remembered that there were two doors on the building: The main door and the door that led outside from the back room with the poker tables and pool tables. Anyone could have opened either of those doors and taken a quick picture of me as I talked to Farrah.

A horrible thought came to me and I had to sit down. Was I defiled now? As far as I knew, only girls got defiled. Girls with bad reputations. I wasn't a girl and I didn't have a bad reputation, even though I wouldn't have minded one. *Could* guys get defiled?

I was just getting up to go and check to see if my picture was posted on the bathroom mirrors when Rick came half running half walking back into the room.

"It's okay," he gasped, like he'd been running. "I checked all the bathrooms. You aren't on the mirrors. You're not defiled." He looked at the creepy photo and pushed it away from him. "At least not yet."

I took a deep breath and then sat back down.

"You should probably drop this case, though," he said. "You've had fair warning."

I nodded. I'd been thinking the same thing.

Part II
FIRE

APRIL

BACK ON

Nothing happened for quite a while. We got through fall term and Christmas break and part of the spring. Dini dated Lester and didn't talk to me, which was okay because I was mostly over her. I kept a low profile so as not to piss off the Defilers, and I worked on my cooking career. Vanessa didn't give me any pressure about continuing the investigation. I think that photo freaked her out. Eventually I stopped thinking about the defilings and the Defiled. For Christmas I asked my grandparents for one of those white smocks and a pair of those black-and-white-checked pants that chefs wear. Fred got me a tall chef's hat and my mom got me some chef's clogs, which are surprisingly comfortable. I wore them once in cooking class. Everyone thought I was joking. I wasn't.

Rick convinced me not to wear my kitchen uniform during regular classes. He said I might never get laid if I did. He obviously doesn't know that chefs are the new race-car drivers, at least as far as sex symbols are concerned.

When Mrs. Samuels saw my chef uniform she teared up a little and told me some long, rambling story about this restaurant she used to work in where the head chef used to throw knives at his assistants when he got mad. Mrs. Samuels says talented chefs can be high-strung, which I figure is evidence that I'm on the right career path.

All in all, ninth grade at Harewood Technical wasn't too bad.

And then it happened.

The first week in April we were making chocolate mousse, which isn't easy, and Rick, who was reading while operating the beater, dropped his book in the bowl and mousse splashed all over me. I headed to the washroom to get it out so I wouldn't have to spend the day looking like a whole flock of birds had crapped in my hair.

Some guys were crowded around the mirror in the big bathroom across from the home ec room. I didn't think much of it until I heard them talking.

"First one this year," said one. "Serves the skank right."

"I heard she's a stone freak," said another one. "She took on half the hockey team in the school van."

"Word is she's diseased. Like bad. You get near her and your dick'll fall off."

"Wouldn't touch that ho with a ten-foot po."

I pushed them aside.

"Watch it, midget," said the rhymer.

I looked at the mirror. A small photo was taped near the bottom right-hand corner.

The first thing that registered with me was that it wasn't Dini. The second thing I realized is that I knew the girl. She was from my old class at Harmack Junior, a fellow ninth grader. Anna Nicholson.

I stared at her smiling face. Anna's one of those girls who's looked old for her age since she was in third grade. She was never exactly pretty, but I always thought she was interesting-looking. She's medium-sized and has curly brown hair. She's got a wide mouth and eyes that seem a little too big for her head, like a cute alien. Anna's family doesn't have much dough. She lives with her dad at her grandma's place, not far from our house. Her mom took off a few years ago after she got involved with drugs and her dad's still messed up over it. Anna is one of those girls who always says the wrong thing and laughs at all the wrong moments. At least, that's what Vanessa says. She wasn't trying to be mean, just explaining why everyone was always so mean to Anna. Vanessa was always nice to her, but most of the other girls couldn't stand her, especially after she started to develop, which she did at about age ten or so.

It seemed like Anna was doing better in high school. At Harewood it didn't matter so much that she looks like a senior. Her skin cleared up and she started using new makeup and got some new clothes or something. I even saw her standing in the Territory one time, waiting to be picked up. Another time I saw her downtown, hanging with a bunch of eleventh and twelfth graders. She looked happy and I was glad for her, because she had a shit time at Harmack Junior and she didn't deserve it.

And now this.

I backed away from the picture and tried to pull myself together. I knew I was going to punch the next guy who spoke.

"What's a matter?" said the bad poet. "You tap that ass? Worried you need a shot now?"

That was all it took. Next thing I knew, hands were grabbing me, pulling me off him.

"Jesus," said the guy as he picked himself off the floor. "Little freak attacked me."

"Maybe that slut's his sister or something," said another guy.

"Well, she's screwed now," said a third and he high-fived his friend.

I turned and ran out of the bathroom before I had to hear any more. I ran straight for the parking lot, I couldn't say why.

I stood in front of the school, right in the middle of the empty Trophy Wife Territory, and looked for her. Where did people go when they got defiled?

An old car pulled out of the teacher's parking lot on the left side of the school. It drove slowly past me. I couldn't see who was driving, but the wild head of curly hair in the passenger side was unmistakable. Anna's head was bent. As I watched, it came up and she looked at me. Her big eyes were red rimmed and raw, her mascara smudged halfway down her cheeks. Her wide mouth was a slash of misery. Our eyes locked and something passed between us. It was like I was the only person in the world who could see her. Like she was asking me to rescue her. And in that instant, I decided I would.

I was back on the case. The Defilers had messed with one of my people and they weren't going to get away with it.

MACK DADDY INVESTIGATIONS, AT YOUR SERVICE

As soon as I got home I lay on my bed to think things through, but my head wouldn't slow down, so I had to get up and walk around. I wanted to tell someone, but was afraid. It was too risky to get my friends involved. The fewer people who knew what I was up to, the better. The thought that I was going to have to go it alone made me extremely lonely. It's hard to take on a big burden without your friends. But it's what investigators do. They fly solo.

I paced around my room a few times, stepping over piles of books and clothes and dishes. Then I thought of something. A book Vanessa gave me a while ago when she was trying to get me to be more logical. It's called *Learn To Be a P.I.*, and to be honest, I never really looked at it, even though I told her it was great.

I found it on one of my bottom shelves and lay down to read it. Turns out it's full of useful information on investigating things. I even sort of enjoyed it. Focusing on the how-to-investigate information stopped me from thinking about Anna's face. That image made me feel a bit suicidal. I couldn't imagine what happened to her to make her look that messed up. I bet there are people who have been shot in the gut who don't look that damaged.

The book talked about the importance of having a good name for your investigative business. You can use either your real name or a made-up name. As soon as I read that, I got this total brain wave. I wasn't going to get cards made up or anything, because my antidefiling operation was going to be conducted strictly on the down low. But I could have a name for myself.

I love the ladies. Vanessa says I mack on them a bit too much. And my name is Sherman Mack. It was perfect. A mack daddy is someone who loves the ladies, but Mack Daddy Investigators love them *and* save them.

Mack Daddy Investigations, at your service.

As soon as I thought of it, I got this whole new confidence. The book was right that a cool name puts a guy in a good headspace.

The book also said that most investigators name their cases as well as their business operations. They often use a code name for privacy. Just like with my professional name, the case name popped right into my head. I'm calling my antidefiling campaign Operation Exposure because that's what I planned to do. I would stop the Defilers by exposing them. I was going to protect the Defiled by making them visible again. At least, that was the plan.

The book said that the key to any covert operation's success can be summed up in one word: surveillance.

It listed quite a few types. There's the hanging around and waiting for a person or suspect kind, which is called *stationary surveillance*. The kind where you follow someone around on foot or in a vehicle (or if you're James Bond, you might follow them in a boat or on skis or whatever) is called *moving surveillance*.

You can do *undercover surveillance* and be very secretive, or you can surveil by being obvious and let people know you're watching them. I'm not sure what the point of that is.

As a new private investigator without too much experience under my belt, I decided to start with stationary surveillance. It seemed like the easiest.

I wasn't sure exactly what happened when someone first got defiled. Would people threaten Anna? Throw rocks through her windows? Put threatening notes under her front door? Or would they start ignoring her right away? I could tell by her face this afternoon that she hadn't just been ignored. Something had happened to her.

I decided that the best plan was to stake out her house. That way I'd be able to protect her and keep an eye out for possible attacks.

That's how I ended up sitting between a big shrub and an even bigger tree in Anna's grandmother's front yard. Unfortunately, I got so excited, thinking about my surveillance, that I forgot to bring certain equipment on the stakeout. The book said you should bring stunners (which is what hip-hop crews call sunglasses), a wide-mouth jar, a newspaper, a cell phone, a credit card, an ice pick, maps, a camera, paper and pencil, binoculars, a simple disguise, and a paperback book to kill time. All I brought was my copy of *Learn To Be a*

P.I., my case log, a pen, and a large bottle of Coke.

The other main problem was that I was sort of nervous and bored at the same time, which I think comes across in my case log notes.

Case Log—Surveillance Transcript
OPERATION EXPOSURE
6:05 P.M.

Now I see why you're supposed to bring a jar. I don't love the idea of going in Anna's yard, even though I am behind a tree. I'm also worried about not having an ice pick. I'm not sure what it would be for, but it doesn't sound like the kind of thing I should have forgotten.

Also the book didn't mention that stationary surveillance would be such a drag. I would give my left 'nad for a Game Boy right now.

Wait! I just heard something. A car pulling up on the street out front. It's times like this I wish I had bionic ears.

OPERATION EXPOSURE
6:17 P.M.

False alarm. It was just some neighbors coming

home. No footsteps up the path to Anna's house. No voices discussing conspiracies. No rescues needed. Nothing. I haven't seen or heard Anna's dad, who's supposedly some kind of shut-in since her mom left, or her grandmother, who has diabetes really bad. I haven't seen Anna, either. I keep thinking about the three of them, each lying in their own dark bedroom. It's a depressing image.

The detectives on *Law & Order* are always complaining about how boring surveillance is, but then two seconds later they see the perp and they chase him and it's pretty exciting. In real life you are bored and uncomfortable and there are bugs on you and you have to go to the bathroom but you can't because you're hiding in the yard of someone you barely even know. A few more of these surveillances and I'll have to write my own book. It will be all about how to deal with the extreme boredom of stationary surveillance.

OPERATION EXPOSURE
6:59 P.M.

When I write my book I'm going to tell people that if they happen to forget their wide-mouth jar, they should pee far enough away from their position so it doesn't ruin their hiding spot.

No wonder Anna's kind of loud when she talks to people. She has to make up for the fact that her house is like a funeral home. Anyone surveilling our house would have seen all kinds of stuff by now—my mom making toast and sewing inappropriate costumes and me closing the blinds before I go on the Internet. Something, anyway.

OPERATION EXPOSURE
7:23 P.M.

Can a person die of boredom? Probably a lot of those unsolved homicides you hear about are actually private investigators who died from how boring surveillance is.

OPERATION EXPOSURE
7:27 P.M.

Surveillance is like being in prison. In solitary confinement. I almost feel like I'm going to go insane. There are probably detainees being held without charge in Guantanamo Bay who are having a better time than me right now.

OPERATION EXPOSURE
7:32 P.M.

I heard that some prisoners try to deal with the loneliness and boredom of imprisonment by making friends with rodents and other vermin. It helps to keep them sane. I haven't seen any rats or mice or anything, but there are ants and beetles all over the place. Also, it's cold as shit.

OPERATION EXPOSURE
7:35 P.M.

It didn't work out with the beetle. Just when I thought we were getting to know each other he crawled under a leaf and wouldn't come out. I wonder if guys in prison run into that problem with their pet rats?

Hey! That reminds me that the other thing people in prison do is work out. I bet there's enough room here to knock off a few sit-ups and get working on my six-pack. I just need to avoid the wet spot.

OPERATION EXPOSURE
7:47 P.M.

The good news is that I just did almost sixty sit-ups.

The bad news is I think I did one on the beetle.

This would be much easier if the Defilers would just stop by right now and leave Anna a threatening note or maybe a Molotov cocktail.

OPERATION EXPOSURE
7:58 P.M.

Still nothing. I wish I could call my friends. Surveillance would be so much better with someone. I wonder what Vanessa's doing right now?

OPERATION EXPOSURE
1:04 A.M.

Oh man, I fell asleep for like four hours! I'm going to have to tear ass out of here to get home before my mom gets home from work. . . . I hope this is one of those nights where she stays out late with the girls.

That's where the first entry in the case log surveillance transcript ends. After rereading it, I don't think I'm the kind of P.I. who should write things down as they happen.

GETTING MADE

After trying out stationary surveillance, I'm thinking that the mobile kind is probably more my style. For one thing, it won't be as boring because you get to move around. For another, if you do stationary surveillance of a girl by yourself when you aren't the police or a certified P.I., people might think you are a pervert as opposed to a concerned and righteous fighter for justice.

When I met up with Rick this morning, I tried to be discreet and anonymous. We walked through the drive-through at Tim Hortons to get coffees. We can't go inside because the bright lights give Rick a headache and his complaining about the bright lights gives me a headache. So instead we get to suck carbon dioxide from all the huge trucks idling in the lineup.

"What happened to you yesterday?" he asked once we'd picked up our coffees and nearly gotten run over about four times.

I'd almost forgotten that I walked out of school the day before.

"Nothing."

"Dude, you didn't come back after you got that stuff in your hair. You left me to do the chocolate mousse on my own. That wasn't cool," he said. "Mousse is hard."

I was feeling quite tense, as well as tired from having spent half the night under a tree, so I wasn't as patient as usual.

"Rick, you think everything we make is hard. It's like you're cooking-challenged or something."

I could tell I had hurt his feelings.

"But you're good at other stuff," I said.

"Well, I couldn't cover for you."

"Whaddya mean? Cover with who?"

"Samuels. She may be a cheerleader but she's not blind. And as soon as she saw the slop I made she knew you weren't around."

"Oh, man," I said.

"I tried. I told her you had a wicked stomach flu. That you cramped up something fierce and had to leave. But she's still looking for you."

He paused and stared at me. "Where'd you go? What did you do last night? I called and messaged you."

I hadn't told anyone about Anna. About the fight in the bathroom. A wave of loneliness came over me. This case was a heavy burden to carry alone.

"I got into something. In the john."

Rick's eyes narrowed.

"What kind of something? Did you spaz again?"

"I didn't spaz. I never spaz. I just get a little mad sometimes, that's all."

"Yeah, like I said. You freak the hell out. Lose it."

Rick was quiet for a moment. "Hey, does this have anything to do with . . ." His voice trailed off. "You know, that thing that happened yesterday? To that girl."

I looked around to see if anyone was listening to us. They weren't. We were about two blocks from school, and there was no one behind us.

I nodded.

"So what happened? How'd you get involved? Because I heard some crazy shit about that girl. Seriously hard-core."

I stopped and stared at him.

"That girl? Her name is Anna. We've gone to school with her since first grade."

"Yeah, but that doesn't mean you know her. If what they say is true you better stay away. And you should stop saying her name. That's the kind of thing that could get you into trouble."

"I'll say her name if I want. Did you ask *her* what happened? Did you talk to her? Or are you just going to let some pictures on a mirror tell you what to do?"

"Sherm, you know . . . her. She's always been kind of, I don't know, sketch. When I heard what she did I felt bad but I believed it."

"What did she supposedly do?"

"Man, I don't want to say. You're all uptight. I know how you get about girls' honor."

I ignored him.

"What did she do?"

Rick sighed and shifted his pile of books under his other arm.

"It's about *who* she did. They say she got wasted at the lacrosse party last weekend. She started coming onto a bunch of guys. Then she took a bunch of them into the back room and, well, you know. Did them."

"Anna wouldn't do that."

"Sherman, she's not exactly self-esteem plus. I can see it happening. And that's not the worst thing."

I waited.

"She made them sick. The guys. They all had to get treated."

He was right. He shouldn't have told me. I had to stop myself from hitting him.

"That's bullshit," I said.

"You don't know that. I'm telling you, Sherm, when I heard it I wasn't totally surprised."

"It's the Defilers putting stuff in your head."

"Everyone says it's true. Have you ever thought that maybe the Defilers only go after the girls that

deserve it? Girls that have already defiled themselves."

I couldn't believe my ears.

"Don't you have sisters? What if this was one of
them?"

"Are you calling my sisters sluts?" Rick didn't
sound upset. He doesn't even like his sisters because
they're sort of tough and they kick him around
quite a bit.

"Even if Anna did do something with those
guys, so what? She doesn't deserve this."

Rick shrugged. "It's the way things work."

"And what if it's all a rumor? How would you
feel then?"

"Bad, I guess."

I decided I wasn't going to protect him anymore.

"Well, get ready to feel bad, then. Because you're
going to help me prove it isn't true."

"What?"

"That's right. I'm launching an investigation
into the case."

"The case?"

"Operation Exposure. We're going to find out who is behind these defilings."

"Wait a minute," he said. "That's not even the point. The point is that she . . . she brought this on herself."

I gave him a fierce look, but he didn't back off. "What if you find out it's true about her?"

"It's nobody's business who she did. But I'm willing to bet that the whole thing is a lie. I'm going to find out what really happened. And you're going to help." I paused. "Oh, and you're not going to mention this to Vanessa. I don't want her getting involved. It's too dangerous."

"What about me?" Rick yelped. "I could get in trouble. Messing with the Defilers."

"*You* brought this on yourself," I said. I thought for a second about whether I'd tell him my private investigator name, but decided he wasn't ready to know it. Yet. I threw my gym bag on his feet.

"Tools of the trade, my friend," I said.

TOOLS OF THE TRADE

Rick wasn't exactly a natural in the private investigator sidekick department. I showed him the surveillance supplies, basically all the things I forgot when I went solo last night. I had to explain everything to him about twelve times.

"What's the jar for?" he asked.

"It's for if you need to, you know . . ."

"Make some jam?"

"No, fool. It's for if you need to go to the can."

"Ever hear of a bathroom? Are you sure this is such a good idea?"

"It's important to maintain a positive attitude when you do mobile surveillance," I said.

"I don't know about this, Sherm. My groin

pull kind of hurts."

"What do you ever do that could pull a groin muscle?"

"I do plenty. Who are we supposed to surveil? Do you even know how to get started?"

"I want to follow up on a few leads. Look for anyone connected to the case. We'll keep an eye out for Anna. Watch the lacrosse players. All you need to do is keep me informed of any sightings."

"Sherm, I don't know anyone who plays lacrosse."

"Look for dudes with facial scars," I said. I thought about what Rick had said about the lacrosse players getting sick from being with Anna. "They might be limping or walking funny."

"From lacrosse?" Then Rick's eyes widened. "Oh!" he said. "You mean if the rumors are true."

I nodded. It was nice not being a solo investigator.

"Take this." I handed him a walkie-talkie.

Neither of us has a cell phone because we are deprived. Walkie-talkies were the best I could do. My grandparents gave me a set a few years ago and I never got to use them much because my mom says she prefers to speak to me in person.

"Dude, these are massive. They look more like boom boxes than walkie-talkies. My groin pull's never going to get better if I have to pack this forty-pound monster around all day." He turned his on and it made a noise like an angry parrot.

"They're classic technology. Anyway, you're only supposed to use it in an emergency."

"Like if I see some guys walking around with a Defiler name tag? Or I see Anna taking on the swim team in the woodworking shop?"

"This isn't a joke, Richard," I said. "Just don't get made."

"Made?"

"Don't you watch *any* TV?"

"My parents put that box on our cable so I can't watch anything with sex or violence."

"Getting made means getting burned."

"Burned?"

"Seen. Don't let anyone catch you watching them."

"Why didn't you just say so?"

Turns out that even with someone helping you,

it's hard to surveil in school. The only people Rick and I surveilled that morning were each other. We tried a quick ten-four check on the radios between first and second period, but some guys from the junior boys' basketball team stole Rick's walkie-talkie and ran all over the school with it pretending to be a SWAT team. Those basketball guys might be tall, but they are even less mature than we are.

Third period I got called to the office. When I got there the secretary sent me to the home ec room to meet with Mrs. Samuels.

Mrs. Samuels was reading *Joy of Cooking*. She's always talking about how it's her favorite book and she reads it like a novel.

"Sherman," she said, very stern.

"Yes, ma'am." I've started calling her ma'am because kitchens are very hierarchical and I might as well get used to it. Plus, I like her. She's pretty decent for a teacher.

"You left class without asking yesterday."

"Yes, ma'am. Sorry, ma'am."

"Would you like to tell me what happened?"

"Rick, I mean Richard, got some mousse on me.

And when I went to the bathroom to wash it off, *wham!* I got pretty sick. Cramped up."

"Did you tell the office? Report to the nurse?"

"No, ma'am. It was one of those where you just want to get home. An emergency."

"I'm afraid that's not good enough. Just because we are both fans of the culinary arts, Sherman, does not mean that you can take advantage."

"No, ma'am."

"When you are in the middle of a dinner service for fifty you'll have to stick it out no matter how you feel."

She sighed and closed *Joy of Cooking*.

"It's a demanding job, Sherman, being a chef. And when you make a mistake in the kitchen there are consequences. Which is why I'm assigning you to detention this afternoon. You'll stay after school for one hour."

I just nodded. I'd stayed out of detention for months. It was too much to expect my good behavior to continue.

At lunch we finally got Rick's radio back by telling the basketball players who had it that it belonged to Coach Little. Then we went looking for suspects. Not being jocks, we had no idea where to find the lacrosse players and Anna hadn't come to school that day, which really wasn't a big surprise. We looked in the cafeteria. I didn't see any lacrosse players, but Vanessa was in there.

She was by herself at one of the big round tables in the cafeteria. We hung back at the doorway, being supercasual and undercover, like the book says. Vanessa kept looking over at us suspiciously.

"Change your hat," I whispered to Rick.

"*You* change your hat. I like this one. It makes me look like Matt Damon."

"It does not. It makes you look like Robin Williams. Anyway, we've got to split up," I said.

"I'm not standing over there," said Rick. He meant the other side of the room, where a bunch of rugby and hockey players were sitting. If he stood near them they'd probably take away his radio, his hat, *and* his chance of ever producing children.

"I've got to be careful of my groin."

It's very difficult to detect with a partner like Rick.

Now Vanessa was staring right at us.

"Vanessa's looking," said Rick.

"I know."

"She's waving us over."

"We're burned," I said.

"Come on, man. It's Vanessa. She's going to think it's weird if you just stand there with that newspaper in front of your face," said Rick.

I let the newspaper fall and folded it as we walked slowly over to her table, trying not to draw attention to ourselves.

"What're you guys doing?" she asked.

"Huh?"

"What were you guys doing over there?"

I looked down at the newspaper in my hand. "Reading. There's a pretty interesting article in here."

"In *Real Estate Weekly*?"

"Yeah. Me and my mom might be moving."

"Really? Where?"

"Down the street. And over."

"What's in the bag?" she asked.

"What bag?"

"The one in your hand, Sherm."

"Oh. This? Just some books and stuff."

"Why didn't you leave it in your locker?"

One thing a detective should know is that girls are abnormally curious. It makes it hard to surveil around them.

"I don't know."

"So what's up with the incognito?" she asked.

Rick and I looked at each other.

"The sunglasses? The hats?"

"We're just feeling kind of private."

She squinted at us. "Did you hear about Anna?" she asked in a voice that should have been much lower.

Rick looked around nervously. "No," he said. He cleared his throat. "And I don't want to."

"She got defiled," said Vanessa. "Yesterday. I heard they got her in the music room. A whole group of people. They threw things at her. A couple of people spat on her."

I thought of Anna's face in the car.

"It's so disgusting," said Vanessa.

"Don't worry," whispered Rick. "Sherm's on it."

"What?" she asked.

"No!" I said. "He's lying." I wanted to keep her out of it.

I shot Rick a glare.

"I'm not," said Rick.

Vanessa got this funny look on her face. "Are you sure that's a good idea?" she asked me.

"I told him it wasn't," said Rick. "I told him to leave it alone."

But Vanessa wasn't listening. "So you're looking into it, Sherm?" she asked. "Even after you got that picture as a warning?"

"It's nothing," I said.

Vanessa stood and picked up her tray. "Well, if you two schmucks are going to investigate, I'll see what I can find out to help."

"It's too dangerous," I said. "Especially for a girl."

She snorted and smoothed her sweater over her hips. Vanessa has great hips.

"Don't worry. I'll be a bit more subtle than you two gomers. I won't hide behind a newspaper in the lunch room."

"I've got it covered," I told her.

"No, *we've* got it covered," she said.

When Vanessa was gone, I turned to Rick. "You are the worst."

"You taught me everything I know."

ARE YOU STILL ENGAGED?

Detention looked exactly the same as it did the first time I went. Four guys and two girls sitting at desks in the classroom across from the office, pretending to read but really just staring into space, waiting for their time to be up. The detention supervisor was a substitute. She looked like she'd just graduated. She was reading a Harry Potter book and wore her hair in braids.

When I walked into the classroom she looked up and told me to sit down. She had a voice like an old blues singer. It freaked me out.

I sat down. Half a minute later, Ed the Head walked in. The substitute didn't say anything to him. He kept his head down and slid into the desk beside me.

His hair covered his face, so I don't think he saw me nod hello.

I wrote a bit on my menu proposal for my dinner party. So far Mrs. Samuels has said that my menu ideas "lack coherence" and "suffer from incongruity," which I think means that I'm mixing stuff that shouldn't go together. Like one menu had shrimp in everything except dessert. I thought people would enjoy that. But Mrs. Samuels said there is such a thing as too much shrimp. Today in detention I brainstormed some ideas for Italian dishes. I was just trying to remember what rigatoni is when the teacher got up, gave us all a harsh glare, said she'd be back in a minute, and then walked out.

I felt a poke in my side. It was Ed, holding an old wooden ruler.

"Little dude," he said, keeping his voice low. His eyes were glassy but alert.

"Hey, Ed."

"How you doing?"

"Good," I said. "You?"

"So you still looking into . . . you know. The shit we talked about last term?"

"Not really," I said, because it was one thing to tell Vanessa and Rick I was back on the case, but I wasn't about to tell Ed.

"You know it happened again, right?" he said. "To another girl."

"Oh, yeah?" I said, very noncommittal.

He pushed his hair back off his face. He had pretty good skin for a guy who spends most of his time locked in a bathroom. I noticed because my skin is a bit acne-fied lately, probably from stress. I may even have to cut down on the cream and sugar in my Tim Hortons if it keeps up. It's one thing to be short and youthful, but short, youthful, and zitty would be too much.

"So they got to you," he said. He smiled and shook his head. "Too bad. You were actually show-ing some stones there for a while."

I didn't say anything.

Ed checked the door of the classroom to make sure the teacher wasn't on her way back and he lowered his voice.

"Now if I was looking into something like that, I'd look for the common denominators," he said. "People who pop up again and again. You dig?"

I nodded, looking straight ahead.

"Like people who used to date defiled people, people who are on the lacrosse team. People like that. What the po po might refer to as 'persons of interest.' A guy spends some time in the bathroom, he hears a few things. Sees things." Ed went quiet for a second. "Hey, kid?"

I turned.

"Is your mom coming to get you?"

I shook my head.

"Shit. I was looking forward to asking her out."

Lucky for me the substitute came back and croaked "Enough talking!" and the small murmurs that had broken out all over the classroom stopped and everything went quiet again.

CLOSING IN

I thought about what Ed the Head said. He was hinting about Lester. It made sense. One of the Defileds had dated Lester. Anna got defiled after allegedly getting busy with the lacrosse team. Lester is the captain of the lacrosse team. We needed to get close to Lester. I didn't tell Rick we were closing in on a specific target until this morning. I knew he would worry, and I was right.

"You want me to watch Lester Broadside?" he said, his voice majorly squeaky.

"And I'll watch Dini."

"Why can't I watch Dini?" asked Rick. "If Broadside catches me following him he'll break my legs."

"Dini might break your legs, too," I pointed out.

"Yeah, but at least she'll look hot while she's doing it," he said. I couldn't argue with that logic.

So we both decided to watch Dini. The good news is we located her pretty fast. We spotted her in the ten-minute break between second and third periods. The bad news is it only took her about two and a half minutes to catch us surveilling her. I probably shouldn't have walked by the open door of the art room so many times. I figured it would be okay because each time I went by I put on a different ball cap.

On my fifth pass, Dini stood in the doorway with her hands on her hips.

"Sherman," she said.

"Yes?" I said.

"What are you doing?"

"Doing?"

She looked past me at Rick, who was holding his position over near the fountain, watching us through his binoculars. When he saw her looking, he ducked into the guys' can.

"You're really starting to freak me out."

A bunch of static burst from my walkie-talkie; then Rick's voice crackled out.

"Sherman, what's happening? Have you made a visual ID of the subject?"

I fumbled, trying to turn off the receiver, and accidentally turned up the volume.

"Sherman. Report your status," squawked Rick's voice. "Are you still engaged with the subject? Any chance you could describe what she's wearing?"

Dini glared from the receiver to me.

Before I could explain, the bell rang for next period. I couldn't think what to do or say, so I just said, "Okay, see you later," and walked away fast.

Surveillance has its dangers. Like if you aren't covert about your surveilling, you might get made by your subject. And then your subject might tell her boyfriend. And then you're screwed.

This all flashed through my mind when Lester pulled his car over beside me as I was walking home from school. I thought about running for it, but decided not to. It was time Lester and I worked this stuff out, *mano y mano*, as they say in Spanish.

He leaned over and spoke through the open passenger window.

"Hey, kid," he yelled over the noise of the engine, which sounded like a gorilla with indigestion.

I frowned to show I wasn't scared, even though, to be honest, I was, a little.

My duffle bag full of surveillance supplies was heavy, but I was glad I had the ice pick with me.

"Get in," he said.

I looked up and down the street. It was empty.

I shook my head, but I tried to do it in a way that seemed brave.

"Come on. I just want to talk to you, kid," Lester said.

He was probably going to throw me off the Nanaimo River bridge. I might live, but I'd be so crippled that I'd never walk, much less detect, again! I got pissed off just thinking about it.

I looked right at Lester. I felt like punching his face in. Just in case, I took off my sunglasses.

"Stop eyeballing me and get in. It's time we had a talk," he said.

I got into his car and put my bag of tools at my feet. I tried to calculate how fast I'd be able to reach the ice pick if I had to.

Lester pulled away from the curb. Inside, the car was still noisy but in this powerfully cool way. Driving in that car was what I imagine it's like to have muscles or a gun: comforting because it's intimidating. If I hadn't been worried about getting capped, I might have even enjoyed it. I could see why Dini liked riding around with Lester.

My hands were shaking a little and I tried to keep them still by hanging on to my knees.

"Relax, kid," he said. "I'm not going to do anything to you. I want to talk about Dini."

My breath sped up. I hated to hear him say her name.

"I know who you are," I said without thinking.

"Excuse me?" He turned to look at me. He really did have excellent hair. Kind of wavy and shiny.

"And I know what you did to your last girlfriend. And to Anna. You better not do that to Dini. Or anyone else, either."

Lester drove with one hand lightly resting on the undersized steering wheel, which he'd wrapped in some kind of white leather.

"What do you know about me and my last

girlfriend?" His voice was permafrost. He wasn't looking at me.

"She got . . . you know. D-listed," I said. "By you. Or you and your lacrosse team."

Lester pulled the car over. I was surprised to see we were in front of my house.

"Look, kid, I have nothing to do with that bull-shit. Me and the guys had nothing to do with what happened to . . . her."

"Her name is Farrah," I said.

Lester breathed out hard, like he was trying to blow out a whole cake full of candles.

"I know her name. And I don't have to explain shit to you. Stop following Dini around, throwing blood at her, and whatever else you've been doing. You're making her nervous."

He drummed his fingers on the steering wheel, which made me think I might be making him nervous, too.

"What are you doing?" he asked.

I gave him the full-on Mack Daddy stare and didn't answer. I wasn't about to conform or deny, or however they say that.

"Look, I'm sorry about what happened to . . . Farrah. I had nothing to do with that. It's different with Dini."

"Oh, yeah? What about all the other girls?"

"What girls?"

"Don't tell me you forgot Anna already."

"Did you OD on your ADD meds, kid? I don't know any Anna."

I was getting a little confused. This was my big confrontation. Shouldn't he be showing some sign of guilt?

I thought back to what Farrah had told me about Lester. How he wasn't made of very good stuff. It was time to change the subject.

"So what if Dini gets defiled too? Are you going to stick by her if she does?"

His face lost some of its movie-dude handsome-ness.

"Look, until it happens to you, to someone you know, you don't get what it's like. The pressure. I have a reputation," he said.

"That's not what I asked," I said.

His chin wasn't as strong as I thought when I

looked at him in profile.

"A man never walks away from his friends," I said.

I may not have a father, but at least I know that.

"Farrah wasn't my friend. She was . . . we were almost broken up."

"That's weak," I said and pushed open the heavy car door.

"Kid—"

I stopped with one foot on the pavement.

"I don't know who did it. Who defiled her. I don't think it was any of the guys on the lacrosse team. I never saw this Anna chick before. You shouldn't stick your nose where it doesn't belong. Defiling is no joke."

I leaned down, shook my head at him, like I was disappointed.

"I mean it about staying away from Dini," he said, but he didn't sound very sure of himself.

I closed the car door feeling like I'd grown about half a foot.

UNPLEASANT AND UNATTRACTIVE CHARACTERS

Being a detective requires boldness. It requires courage. And sometimes, it means mixing with unpleasant, unattractive characters, such as Coach Little. On Monday afternoon, I steeled myself and walked into his office, after spending most of the weekend trying to decide what to do. I walked by Anna's house about twelve times, but she seemed to have disappeared. I read *Learn To Be a P.I.* and decided that I had to get close to the lacrosse team, who were the next logical suspects. They knew Lester and presumably Farrah, and everyone was saying that Anna had been with at least one of them before she got D-listed. I wasn't going to take Lester the Molester's word for it that the lacrosse team were not the Defilers. Sometimes you have to dance with the devil to . . . you know, find evil people.

"Excuse me, Coach Little?" I said.

He looked up from whatever he was doing. He hadn't gotten any better-looking over the weekend. His face was very red, like he'd just been released from a choke hold that had cut off most of the oxygen supply to his brain.

"What?"

Damn, his teeth were yellow. Why do the worst teachers always have the most terrible teeth? Someone should do a study.

"I was wondering, sir . . ." I nearly choked on the last word. "I was wondering if you needed any help with the lacrosse team?"

Coach Little narrowed his eyes and bared his indented teeth at me. "Help?" he asked, rising out of his seat a little. "Help?"

I stepped back. "I don't mean help with coaching or anything. I just mean, like, general assistance."

I probably should have researched lacrosse before

volunteering. I don't know anything about lacrosse except that the players' parents always seem to have lacrosse stickers on their minivans.

"I could help with maintaining the equipment," I said.

"Why?"

"So I could get more, you know, involved in sports. I've been working on my, you know, abs and . . ." I made the mistake of looking at his face. It was purple with disgust. It would have been easier to try and join the Hells Angels than get Coach Little to let me join the lacrosse team.

"Look, Mack. You want to get involved in a sport, why don't you try track or something?"

He didn't sound quite as mean as he usually does. Maybe his skin was just naturally that purplish color.

"Or table tennis," he kept on. "One of those sports that's good for little guys. Lacrosse is a rough game."

I was about to argue with him when a couple of guys from the lacrosse team walked in, huge in their royal blue and yellow team jackets with the

SUSAN JUBY

lacrosse patches on the back.

"Hey, Coach," said one. "You know we're having a team barbecue at my mom and stepdad's place in the north end this weekend. We were wondering if we could bring Thor."

Thor is the giant lacrosse stick the lacrosse team uses as its mascot. They are probably not mature enough to look after an actual, live animal such as a goat or a sheep.

Coach Little grunted and thumbed behind him to where Thor leaned against the wall. The stick nearly touched the ceiling.

"You gonna stop by, Coach?" asked the bigger of the two.

"No. I'm taking the girls' wrestling team to a meet in Port Hardy."

I may not be a jock, but I had exactly the same question about the girls' wrestling team that they did.

"Do the girls wear those little shorts?" one asked.

"Shut it, Featherstone. And, Kelsey, you better bring back that stick in one piece."

All through this, I'd been trying to be as quiet

and still as possible. When the lacrosse guys turned to leave, the one called Featherstone bumped me with his shoulder, knocking me into the door frame.

"That it, Mack?" said Coach Little, his gaze following his players and then coming back to rest on me.

"Yeah, that's it," I said.

DISINFECTED YOUTH

The bad news is that I couldn't get anyone from my crew to come out on surveillance with me even though I spent all week trying to convince them. They even acted almost like they weren't my crew. Vanessa had to go to a birthday party. I always forget that Vanessa has girlfriends. She has a way of making you feel like you're her only friend—or at least her best friend—when you're with her, so I'm always surprised that she's got this whole life that's not about me.

Rick was at some church slideshow with his parents. It started at six o'clock. Rick figured he wouldn't get out of there until ten at the earliest.

Ashton had a private art class with a painter who

was visiting his parents.

That meant that I was on my own with locating and investigating the lacrosse party and trying to find clues to the defilings. The good news is that you can find out the location of any north end party, even if it's just two people playing Halo and eating pizza, if you hang around outside Mac's, a twenty-four-hour convenience store in the north end of town. It's near the end of Long Lake, where a lot of kids from the north end party. If the lacrosse guys came through here on their way to the barbecue, I'd be on them like Velcro on . . . well, Velcro, I guess.

I know from reading Vanessa's detective novels and watching crime shows that private dicks spend a lot of time driving around looking for people. They drive from interview to interview. They drive around and think deep and often depressing thoughts about life. They drive to meet women they're sleeping with. The key thing is that they have wheels.

Unfortunately, driving wasn't an option for me, and getting my mom to drive me around would bone my image.

My mom backed over my bike a few months
ago so that left me with Miss Piggy, the pink cruiser
bike my mom bought herself last year so she could
cross train for her dancing. She rode it around the
block a few times and then never touched it again.
Miss Piggy is bright pink and has radical swoopy
handlebars and a metallic pink fender with daisies
painted on it. Before I rode it over to the mall, I cut
the ribbons off the handlebars, but that didn't help.
Miss Piggy doesn't have any gears or hand brakes or
anything, so not only is it girly, but it's also dangerous. Still, Miss Piggy is all I've got for doing vehicu-
lar surveillance outside Mac's on a Saturday night.

I immediately noticed one drawback about doing
surveillance on a bike. It's hard to balance a report
log and coffee on the handlebars. (All detectives
drink coffee during their stakeouts. Luckily, Mac's
has a bathroom, so I didn't have to deal with the jar
on top of everything else.)

I felt a little exposed, even though I had parked
Miss Piggy between two Dumpsters. The north
end of town is where all the newer houses and most
of the malls and stuff are. There are a lot of malls

in this town. The local joke is that the word *Nanaimo* means "Land of Many Malls."

You'd think, since a lot of north end kids are more privileged and have more shopping opportunities than those of us in the south end, they'd be nicer than less advantaged youth such as myself, but that is mos def not the case. I've seen more hostile forces in the half hour I've been hiding here than I would in a whole night parked outside the Salvation Army thrift store near our place.

In some parts of the south end, there'd be more obvious drug addicts and drunks wandering around. But they'd be so busy drinking and doing drugs and forgetting their kids in the car while they went to the casino they wouldn't have time to menace random dudes like me. Here in the north end, half the kids I'd seen at that point were dressed like gangbangers. I felt like a Blood in Crip territory, and the pink bike wasn't helping my confidence much.

If I tried hiding between two Dumpsters in my neighborhood, ten single mothers on welfare would have come charging out of their houses, all wool socks and Birkenstocks, asking me what I was doing, maybe trying to get me to come in for tea or getting me in touch with a social worker, which our neighborhood has a lot of because of all the drunks and drug addicts. But out here in the 'burbs, I'm invisible. People have parked two inches from me in their Lexuses and their Tahoes and not noticed me. No wonder the teens here are so, you know, disinfected, or whatever they call it when kids are bad.

My plan was to watch for people wearing lacrosse jackets. I would walk past them, real casual like, overhear the party location, and then follow them at a safe distance on my bike. Once I reached the party, I wasn't sure what I'd do. Probably hide in the yard. Or maybe break into their cars to find evidence. I wish I knew what I was looking for. A defiling in progress would be nice.

Staking out a large target like Mac's was not for cowards. The fish and chips restaurant in this plaza puts their garbage in one of the Dumpsters I was hiding beside and the smell was way serious.

By the time I'd been parked between these two Dumpsters for forty-five minutes, my nerves were

JACKED

"Hey, kid," said a tall guy. "What are you doing back there?"

I tried to look casual. I leaned against the rotten fish–smelling blue Dumpster, as if it was completely normal for me to be hanging out there. Like pretty much any above-average young guy my age would want to spend some quality time hiding between Dumpsters on his mom's pink bicycle in the Mac's parking lot.

I sort of shrugged, which wasn't that easy, since I was leaning on the Dumpster.

The tall one's friend had long, blond hair. He shook his hair and for a second I got a look at his face, which was otherwise pretty much hidden.

He didn't look too tough. Tougher than me, yes. But not *that* tough.

"You some kind of pervert?" asked the tall guy. He said it like he was just curious and it was not a problem if I was.

I'd backed up so far, I was almost sitting in the hedge that divided the Mac's parking lot from the sidewalk and the street. With the hedge behind me, Dumpsters on either side, and the two guys in front, I was trapped.

Investigators who drive cars are really lucky. Sure, sometimes criminals sneak up and shoot them while they're on a stakeout, but that has quite a bit more masculine pride to it than being trapped between two Dumpsters with your pink girl bike. If I had a car right then, I'd have driven away.

I was glad these guys weren't being too threatening, although one of them was wearing a fairly threatening aftershave. It even cut through the smell of rotten fish.

I sneezed and felt stupid.

"Bless you, homes," said the tall guy. The blond guy nodded.

The tall one took a sip of his giant Slurpee cup.

The blond one swept his hair out of his eyes with one thumb. It was a pointless thing to do, since his hair just went right back into his eyes.

"You steal that bike?" asked the tall guy. The blond one didn't seem like much of a talker. Maybe because his hair got in his mouth if he opened it.

I shook my head again, trying for cool and casual.

"It's my aunt's." For some reason I figured that sounded better than "it's my mom's."

"Can I see it?" asked the tall guy.

"Uh, okay."

I pushed Miss Piggy toward him.

He pulled the bike out from between the Dumpsters.

He held it by the handlebars and moved it back and forth like he was checking something mechanical. The bike looked cooler in his hands.

"Mind if I take her for a spin?" the tall guy asked.

I was starting to like him. He was a decent guy.

"Sure," I said.

He swung a leg over Miss Piggy and rode her in big, easy circles around the Mac's parking lot.

I was so busy watching him that I didn't notice

the blond guy pick up his BMX, which had been out of sight behind him. One second he was standing, the next he was pedaling like a madman after the tall guy who was pumping toward the parking lot exit on my mom's pink bike.

I ran out from between the two Dumpsters to see the two guys heading north on Ross Road.

"Hey!" I called after them. It was the best I could do on short notice.

That would have been embarrassing enough, but then I heard giggling.

"Hey yourself," said a girl's voice. "Did those guys just steal your bike?"

"Sweet ride, too," said another female voice, gravelly and sexy.

It was getting so dark I had to squint my eyes to see Vargo Tremaine and Clarissa Kim, top Trophy Wives, standing on the sidewalk across from the Dumpsters.

How much had they seen? Was there any way to save face in this situation? Could they tell I'd been working on my abs? Probably not.

I stepped toward them and brushed what I

hoped wasn't a piece of rotten fish off my sleeve.

I smiled. It probably looked like something you'd see on the face of a dog hoping not to get kicked.

"What were you doing in between those Dumpsters?" asked Vargo. She seemed very amused. Or as amused as someone who is made up to look like she died a few hours earlier can look. Her leather collar gleamed softly in the moonlight.

"Uh, sorry?" I said, pretending I had no idea what she was talking about.

I was glad it was dark so the girls couldn't see my face turn hot and red and guilty.

"What were you doing over by the Dumpsters?" Vargo asked again.

"I was, uh . . ." My voice went so high probably only dogs could hear it. I tried again. "I was, ah, looking for a, you know, party."

Clarissa grinned at me. Huge smile. Gleaming.

"Any specific party?" she asked.

"What were you *really* doing in between those Dumpsters?" said Vargo, who would probably make a very good private investigator.

I tried to act like I didn't know what she was talking about. Like I'd just been strolling along and happened to end up between the Dumpsters. Like that spot was a major destination for happening-type guys.

Both girls stared at me. Their combined hotness and older-womanness was making me sweat. It's impossible to relax in this world due to all the women everywhere looking hot and asking questions and making me worry about everything.

"I was waiting," I said.

"For what?" asked Vargo.

I cleared my throat. "I was keeping watch," I said. "Surveilling."

"You planning to rob Mac's? 'Cause I don't see you doing well in the joint," said Clarissa. She's a high school girl who doesn't know any more about prison than I do. But because she's so good-looking and cool, it doesn't matter what she says. You totally believe it.

"I am looking out for a friend," I said, realizing I should keep my mouth closed. "I'm kind of conducting an informal investigation."

"Who's this friend?" asked Clarissa. "Is it a girl?"

I nodded.

"What's her name?"

Now I was stuck.

"She's just a girl."

"There is no such thing as just a girl," said Vargo. "What's her name?"

My mind raced and my mouth followed it. "She got in a little trouble recently. I'm trying to help her out."

Vargo's eyes narrowed, making them look even more catlike. She made a "come on" gesture with the fingers of her right hand.

"Her name's Anna," I said.

Vargo's pierced eyebrows went up. Even Clarissa looked shocked.

"You mean that girl who got . . . you know, last week?"

I nodded and felt instantly better. Why was it such a relief to tell people what I was doing? I was the least-private private detective ever.

"Poor kid," said Clarissa. The look of sympathy on her pretty freckled face seemed real.

"God, I hate that stuff," said Vargo. "It's the worst thing about going to Scarewood."

Now I was confused. These were two of the most powerful people at Harewood. If they didn't like defiling, why did they go along with it?

"So you're looking into *defiling*?" said Clarissa.

"On your own?" said Vargo. "Wow."

I felt a flush of pride.

"Aren't you worried you're going to get in trouble?" asked Clarissa.

All at once I got it. They were just as afraid of getting defiled as everyone else in the school. Just as afraid of ending up on the mirror. Of being talked about. Socially destroyed. Disappeared.

"Do you believe what they say about them?" I asked. "That they asked for it?"

"Maybe," said Clarissa.

"Does it matter?" said Vargo, turning to Clarissa. "A girl should be able to make mistakes without getting her life ruined."

She ran a finger over her collar and looked thoughtful.

"So what are you doing?"

"I'm just trying to figure out what happened.

To Anna. I heard it had something to do with the lacrosse team." I paused, then took a chance. "And Lester Broadside."

"I dig his hair," said Clarissa.

"I've heard some stuff about him, though," said Vargo.

My heart jerked in my chest.

"What stuff?"

"That girlfriend of his from last year. She got hit with the big D," said Vargo. She looked at Clarissa. "Remember that girl last year? The tenth grader. Farrah or something?"

Clarissa crinkled her nose, trying to remember.

"She's a total mess now. People said she got D-listed by Lester and his friends."

"That's so negative," said Clarissa.

"I know. I'd think twice before going near him, no matter how good his hair is."

Vargo looked at me. "How old are you, anyway? Aren't you kind of young to be doing Dumpster surveillance at night?"

I didn't answer. I was offended. Also, this conversation was all over the place. I couldn't keep up. Talking to Vargo and Clarissa was like trying to talk to my mom, only worse, due to the fact that they are hot.

"I started staying out late when I was twelve," said Clarissa, in her raspy voice. "Are you twelve yet?"

I stared at her, extremely offended now. I'm definitely going to stop wearing sunscreen. If I am ever going to be taken seriously as a man, I need to work on my abs and on getting more wrinkles.

"I'm not twelve," I said, standing up on my toes to add a bit to my height. "I'm nearly fifteen. I'm in ninth grade."

"I think it's great that you're looking out for your girlfriend," said Vargo to me, her voice softer now.

"Who's your girlfriend?" said Clarissa, whose short-term memory has obviously been impaired by drug use.

"She's not my girlfriend," I said.

"Who *is* your girlfriend?"

This was embarrassing.

"Cutey like you must have a girl," said Clarissa.

I thought of Dini. She definitely wasn't my girlfriend. Then Vanessa's face popped into my head.

"Look at his face!" said Vargo. "It went all moony there for a second!"

I frowned.

"He's got a girl." Clarissa gave a raspy, happy laugh. "Right on," she said.

I was drowning in this conversation.

"She's just a friend."

"Does she know what you're up to?" asked Vargo.

I nodded, thinking of how impressed Vanessa had looked when I told her I was going to start investigating again.

"I bet she thinks you're all chivalrous and brave," said Vargo.

She was so intense she was freaking me out. "That is so sweet of you," she added, still all up in my space. "She's lucky to have you."

"Totally," said Clarissa.

I felt myself grow at least an inch and my abs get more rocklike. Finally, I'd found some ladies who appreciated my potentialities!

"Now tell us again why you were hiding behind

those Dumpsters?"

"I'm looking for the lacrosse team barbecue. I'm going to stake it out." I took a deep breath, not sure I could trust these girls, and then decided, *What the hell.* If I was going to be betrayed, it might as well be by some fine foxes.

"That's where we're going!" said Clarissa, practically jumping up and down like a little kid.

"And we will take you there," said Vargo.

"This is going to be so cool. We'll all go to the lacrosse party together. It's like destiny," said Clarissa. "What was your name again?"

"Sherman."

"Like the tank," said Vargo.

"This is just so awesome," said Clarissa. Before I knew what was happening, she and Vargo hugged me and I was in danger of fainting again.

"I wish every guy was as awesome as you," said Clarissa after they let me go.

Clarissa Kim may not know a lot of adjectives, but she smells fantastic. Like pot and clothes that have been hung out to dry on a line.

"Come on, Sherman, we'll help you," said Vargo.

"I've always hated that defiling bullshit."

She led me over to where two brand-new scooters were parked. She handed me a silver motorcycle helmet.

"You can ride with me as long as you don't mind sharing with Guido."

Guido was the naked full-sized blow-up doll she had tied to the back of her scooter. All I knew was that I wasn't on a pink bike anymore and I got to put my arms around Vargo. A minute later we were cruising out of the Mac's parking lot.

Sometimes, getting your bike jacked is the best thing that can happen to a person.

WITH A LITTLE HELP FROM MY (HOT) FRIENDS

Vargo and Clarissa pulled over outside a large house. About six or seven cars were parked in the driveway and down the street. None of the cars were parked on the lawn, which was a relief because I know from watching teen movies that's a sure sign a party has gone out of control and is about to be busted up by the cops. One of the cars was definitely Lester's.

After I got off the scooter and let go of Vargo, it dawned on me that the situation wasn't ideal. My plan had been to be invisible at the party, but here I was, walking up with two of the hottest ladies in school. Everyone knows that good-looking girls are the most visible people on the planet.

"Fun, eh?" said Vargo.

"I didn't know you had your own wheels," I said.

"We decided smart girls should have their own wheels," said Vargo.

"Where are your boyfriends?" I asked, just in case I was going to have to deal with jealous dudes.

"They had other plans." Vargo tucked Guido under her arm. "You know, Sherman, just because people call us Trophy Wives doesn't mean we actually are."

I blinked, not quite catching her meaning.

"We like to think of our men as Trophy Husbands. And tonight, you're our Trophy Date."

My face and a few other parts became warm, and Vargo and Clarissa laughed. They started toward the house and I tugged on Vargo's sleeve.

"Just a second," I said.

Vargo and Clarissa turned to me. I had this moment of wishing I was Guido and that I could hide under Vargo's arm.

"I was wondering. Well, actually, the thing is. I, uh . . ."

"Spit it out, Sherm," said Clarissa, who is so physically brave that she doesn't have any concept of how the rest of the world lives. Of course, it probably helps that she smokes about two round bales of dope every day.

"Are you afraid to go in there?" asked Vargo, leaning forward so I could smell her perfume. It was sort of spicy and sweet, like secrets. It mixed with the plastic smell of Guido in a way that was surprisingly enjoyable. I could practically feel a new scent fetish forming.

Instead of trying to pretend I wasn't afraid, I tried something completely new. The truth.

I nodded.

Clarissa and Vargo seemed to like that. Their faces went all gentle and sympathetic and best of all Vargo *did* tuck me under her other arm. She squeezed me so that I ended up almost kissing Guido's plastic, round-mouthed face, which I didn't even mind much because Clarissa joined us for another hug. This group hugging was probably the closest I was ever going to get to a threesome.

After the extremely excellent clinch broke up,

Clarissa stepped back and looked at the house.

"This is Ben Kelsey's mom's house," she said. "I've been to parties here before. We can go in the back door. Everyone will be in the kitchen or the living room. We'll make sure no one sees you."

"He wants to be able to watch. So he can find clues," said Vargo.

"We'll be his eyes and ears," said Clarissa. "I always wanted to go undercover. One of us will stay with Sherm, the other one will watch for any sign of negative, D-listing-type activity."

Five minutes later I was sitting in Ben's mother's big walk-in closet, surrounded by MILF-wear— high-heeled shoes on wire racks and clothes that smelled like flowers. I was disappointed to see that Mrs. Kelsey didn't keep her really personal stuff in the closet. You know, panties and bras and whatnot. I have sort of a fetish about them, too, thanks to my mother's taste in art. If I ever went to jail I would be one of those prisoners who lives for the day the Victoria's Secret catalog gets delivered.

Clarissa and Vargo left me alone while they went to scope out the party. That gave me time to worry about how many new fetishes I was getting. Plastic, underwear, aprons—I'm pretty much abnormally interested in all of them.

Clarissa came back ten minutes later, and she brought Raquel George, the third top-tier Trophy Wife with her.

"Oh, hi!" said Raquel, like we were good friends and she'd been hoping to run into me in the closet.

"I told Raquel what you're doing," said Clarissa. "She's supportive."

"And I'm bored. Tal won't stop playing poker long enough to pay any attention to me."

I tried to look manly, like there was steel in my jaw and I wasn't freaked out that Clarissa was telling everyone what I was doing here. It was hard, because there were a bunch of silky blouses brushing the top of my hair, which for some reason made me feel like I was wearing underpants on my head.

"So you're investigating Lester and the lacrosse team," said Raquel.

I nodded. I was feeling kind of sweaty due to being in a closet with three Trophy Wives.

Raquel looked around. "Nice place you got here, Sam," she said.

"Sherman," I said.

"Anyone want to help me smoke this?" asked Clarissa, fingering a joint.

Raquel waved a hand in a "sure, whatever" gesture. "So, Sherman. Tell me more about your investigation," she said.

"Sherm thinks Lester and the lacrosse guys might be the Defilers." Clarissa spoke through teeth clenched around the joint while she felt around in her low-slung cargo pants for her lighter. "One of the girls from his old elementary school just got D-listed. He heard it had something to do with the lacrosse team."

"No way," said Raquel, looking fascinated. "What happened?"

Clarissa puffed out a cloud of smoke.

"The usual. Her picture went up. People said she's been whoring around with some guys. That she's one big STD. Everyone stopped talking to her. I've never actually seen her myself."

"So was she?" asked Raquel.

I looked at her. Something about the slightly hungry look around her mouth made me nervous.

"Was she what?" asked Clarissa.

"Whoring around. From what I hear, the girls on that list are all asking for it," said Raquel. "I mean, that's what they say. I don't agree with it, of course."

Her cat eyes rested on me. "A little sluttery is not necessarily a bad thing." She smiled, showing wet and shiny teeth. "So this girl, was she your girlfriend?"

I shook my head.

"No," said Clarissa. "But he's investigating this for his girlfriend. He's trying to impress her."

"Wow," said Raquel. "You're brave. Defiling is some serious shit. No one messes with the system."

"I don't really have a girlfriend," I said.

"A very brave boy," repeated Raquel, ignoring what I'd said. Then she gave me a whole new kind of look that I couldn't quite figure out. It was almost like interest.

I looked from Clarissa Kim to Raquel George and wished my friends could see me now.

IF THE SHOE DOESN'T FIT

"So what's the plan?" asked Raquel when Vargo came back to the closet to tell us she hadn't seen anything suspicious except lacrosse players shotgunning beer.

"I tried asking if there was anything new with the team lately," said Vargo. "But no one seemed to know what I was talking about. And I wasn't about to bring up the girl directly. I don't want to end up on the mirror."

The other two nodded seriously. It was hard to believe that even Trophy Wives were afraid of being defiled.

"It's okay," I said. "You probably shouldn't get involved. This is my case." I said the last word quietly because it was a little embarrassing to say it out loud.

The girls ignored me.

"We'll take turns," said Vargo. "One of us will stay close to Lester and the rest of the guys, in case they say something incriminating. The other two will stay here with Sherm. Who wants to go outside next?"

"I'll take a turn, once I finish this," said Clarissa, holding up the joint. The closet was thick with smoke. I think I was getting a contact high, or whatever that kind of high is where you get wasted without touching any drugs. This smell was totally going to get in my clothes. My mom would recognize it, too. That's one of the drawbacks of having an abnormally youthful parent. She is able to identify illegal activities since she only stopped doing them like two weeks ago.

After Clarissa left, Vargo sat down across from me. She swung the closet door open and closed a few times to air it out while Raquel tried on Ben Kelsey's mother's shoes. There was a mirror at the end of the closet and Raquel kept model-walking up to it, turning and walking back.

"These are wicked," she said, lifting one of her

feet to show us a glossy red high heel with ankle
straps.

Vargo leaned forward and stared at me again,
like I was a corpse she was about to dissect.

"Sherman," she said. "I'm still not completely
clear why you're doing this."

I blinked. I shrugged. Then I decided to try a
little more truthfulness, since it worked so well last
time.

"It just, you know, doesn't seem right."

"And you're trying to impress your girlfriend."

"She's not my girlfriend."

"But you wish she was."

I nodded.

"Sherman, are you a horndog?" asked Vargo,
like she was asking what my sign was.

"He's definitely a horndog," said Raquel,
pulling on a pair of heels made completely of clear
plastic.

"Maybe a little," I said. "But I'm not dangerous
or anything."

Vargo and Raquel both looked at me.

What is it about girls? They dig it when you're

even the littlest bit honest about how weak you are. Do other guys know this? My friends definitely don't. Rick lies to every girl he meets about everything. He says girls expect it. Now that I've tried truth a few times, I'm convinced it's the way to go.

"I'm not just doing it for my friend," I said. "The whole defiling thing is wrong."

Vargo nodded, her perfect face serious. "Word," she said, and she didn't even sound like a tool saying it. She leaned back against the wall of the closet and stared at the ceiling as she spoke. "So you are single-handedly going to stop the defilings?"

I shrugged. "I guess. I just want to find out who's doing it."

"You've got some serious stones for a guy your age," said Vargo.

I liked it when she said that.

Raquel sat down right beside me and my stomach did a slow flip.

"You're cute," she said. "Too bad you're so young."

I tried not to think of her giant boyfriend playing poker in another room in the same house. I said a little prayer that his money would hold out and he wouldn't come looking for Raquel.

She stretched her legs out beside mine, so close they were nearly touching. She still had on the clear plastic heels.

"Hey! Our feet are almost the same size," she said, pointing.

This wasn't as bad as it sounds, because Raquel is at least a foot taller than I am. My feet are proportionally quite large.

"Do you think you could walk in shoes like these?" she asked.

I shrugged. I was having trouble breathing. Sometimes I think I might die of girls. Like one will get too close and I'll just be over.

"Let's try," she said, reaching over and grabbing a pair of silver heels from a wire rack.

Vargo smiled at us but didn't say anything.

"Come on. Take off your shoes," said Raquel.

I wasn't about to argue. Raquel is a take-charge girl and I like take-charge girls.

"Put them on."

I stuck my toes into the right shoe.

"It's too small," I said, relieved.

"You've got to take off your socks," said Raquel.

"I don't know about—"

"Come on! It will be fun. It's getting so boring in here."

I didn't want them to be bored, so I took a deep breath and peeled off my socks. I was glad I had on clean ones with no holes. Courtesy of my grandparents, who sometimes put six-packs of tube socks in with our vitamin-and-fruit baskets.

The shoes were tight, but I could get them on. They felt like little prisons for my toes.

"Can you walk in them?" asked Raquel.

What the hell, I thought. What will it hurt?

I pushed myself up. One of the heels twisted underneath me and I nearly fell over.

"These are brutal," I said as I walked across the closet. "They're like torture devices."

"We suffer to be beautiful," said Raquel.

Vargo snorted. I think she just suffers as a matter of principle.

"Okay, walk toward me. Like you're a model," said Raquel.

I wobbled toward her and she clapped her hands, excited, like she was watching a baby take its first steps.

"The patriarchy invented high heels," said Vargo.

"Ben Kelsey's dad makes shoes?" I asked, half sitting, half falling down.

Vargo rolled her eyes.

Raquel moved closer to me. "Would it be sick if I kissed him?" she asked Vargo.

This was getting so weird. And great.

I crossed my legs so neither girl would see what I thought of Raquel kissing me. I stared directly into one of the lights.

"I'm sure that would be fine," I croaked, and closed my eyes. When I did that Vanessa's face floated into my mind, but I quickly pushed it out of there.

"We're in a closet, Raquel," said Vargo. "Do what you need to do."

"You know what would be hot?" said Raquel, leaning right into me, her soft chest pressing into my arm and messing me up severely in ways I can't even name. "If you put on some of Mrs. Kelsey's clothes. Then we could make out with you. It would be like a form of sexual experimentation."

When she put it that way it sounded like a good idea.

"Here, try this," said Raquel, reaching up and grabbing something shiny and blue from a hanger overhead.

I thought about saying no. About being truthful again. But this didn't seem like the right time.

I looked from Raquel to Vargo.

"Go ahead. Put it on," said Raquel.

Like a hypnotized person, I undid the Chinese knot–style buttons at the neck and pulled the blouse on. As soon as I got it over my head and poked my arms through the sleeves I realized with a panicky feeling that I wasn't going to be able to get it off.

I tried to pull it back up. It took my T-shirt with it, totally exposing my non-ripped abs.

"Don't wreck it!" said Raquel.

I heard the closet door open. I couldn't see who it was because my face was trapped in the blouse.

"Could someone please tell me why he's wearing a blouse on his head and silver shoes on his feet?"

SUSAN JUBY

I pulled the blouse down so my stomach could have some privacy.

"I can't believe you didn't wait for me," said Clarissa.

"What's going on out there?" I asked, trying to take everyone's mind off the fact that I was stuck in a woman's blouse.

"Never mind *out there*. I want to know what's going on in here," said Clarissa.

"We are exploring our feminine power," said Raquel.

Vargo moved over to sit next to me. She put a bare arm around my shoulders, which were bulging out of the blue satin shirt. Before I knew what was happening Vargo turned and kissed me, half on my mouth, half on my cheek. I froze. Well, most of me froze. One part refused.

I squeezed my eyes shut, trying to get control of all my parts.

Next thing I knew, Raquel's chest was pressed into my arm again. She used her hand to turn my face to hers and started kissing me. The smell! And the softness. I was going to explode. I crossed my

189

legs and put my hands over my crotch.

They pulled away.

I could feel all three girls staring at my hands. They knew what I was hiding. I tried to think of dead cats. Of Coach Little. Finally, I thought of Anna's face in the car as she drove by and the pressure started to ease.

Raquel, Clarissa, and Vargo all wore small, satisfied smiles.

I cleared my throat and moved my hands to my knees, trying to keep a bit of masculine pride.

"Did you see anything suspicious out there?" I asked in a voice even I didn't recognize.

Clarissa shrugged. "The boys are just getting loaded and playing with that big lacrosse stick. They haven't said anything. No one's mentioned the defiled girl."

"Okay. Well, I guess I'll take my turn now," said Raquel. She leaned over and kissed me once more. Right on the mouth. I put my hands back between my legs.

Thirty seconds later she was gone and I was trying to work one of my elbows through an armhole when Vargo's phone buzzed.

"Yes?"

Her face went still as she listened.

"What? When? Okay, we'll be there soon."

She closed her phone and jumped up, all vinyl and fishnets.

"We have to go," she said.

Who did she mean by *we*?

"Pete wiped out on his scooter. He's at the hospital. Randy's with him. They were together."

"But they don't usually hang out," said Clarissa.

"I don't know how it happened, but we've got to go. Now."

Vargo looked at me. "Sherm, stay here until Raquel gets back. She'll sneak you out."

Then they were gone and I was alone in the closet. I pulled off the silver shoes and returned them back to the rack.

Of all my surveillances so far, this one had definitely been the craziest.

A BRUCE WILLIS MOMENT

Five, then ten minutes passed and I was still sitting alone. Raquel hadn't come back to get me and I was facing not only my usual problem on stakeout (that last coffee outside Mac's had been a mistake) but also genuine danger. Ben Kelsey would kill my ass if he found me in his mom's closet. Especially if he found me wearing her blouse, which I couldn't seem to get off without tearing it. Every time I got it halfway over my head and started to raise my arms I heard a ripping sound under the sleeves. I was either going to have to cut it off, or get some help. Maybe there was some special technique girls use to get their tight blouses off.

I kept hearing people from the party come in and out of the room to use the bathroom. Every time the toilet flushed, my bladder went into spasms.

Finally, I couldn't take the pressure from my bladder anymore. I cracked open the door of the closet. The bathroom across from me looked empty.

I poked my head out farther, glanced both ways, and ran for it, carrying my shoes so I'd be as soundless as possible. As soon as I hit the bathroom I slid the door shut and locked it after me.

I was just finishing when someone tried to open the door. I went still. The person on the other side jiggled the handle once more.

"Are you going to be long?" asked a girl's voice.

Using the kind of quick thinking that private investigators depend on, I grabbed a towel and used it to muffle my voice.

"Yeah," I said, sounding like a kidnapper calling about a ransom payment. "Number two."

"Gross!" said the voice.

But it worked and she split.

After a few minutes I assumed I was alone again. I thought about trying to wait out the party in the bathroom, but I knew people would start to wonder who was in there. What if Ben Kelsey's mom and stepdad came home? They might not like finding me in their personal bathroom.

I took a deep breath and opened the door. All I could see was the massive bed. It was nearly the same size as our entire living room. The fluffy white bedspread matched the fluffy white carpet exactly, and so did the fluffy white pillows. The entire room looked like the inside of a bag of cotton batting. Or a rich person's insane asylum. Maybe that's why my mom loves red walls. There is such a thing as too much white.

I stepped out of the bathroom and ran around the bed and then threw myself behind the doorway. It was a total Bruce Willis moment. As soon as it seemed safe, I looked out and down the hallway. The coast was clear.

Without stopping to think, I made a break for it, still hanging on to my shoes. I made it halfway down the corridor, headed, I hoped, for the back door of the house, when I passed an open doorway. From the corner of my eye I caught a flash of movement. A second later I was flying through the air. And then I wasn't. Of the two, flying through the air is better.

COLD COCKED

In Vanessa's crime novels, the private detectives and cops are always getting ambushed and hit on the head. They wake up minutes or hours later with no memory of who they are or what happened to them. As far as I'm concerned, those guys got lucky.

I only *wish* I couldn't remember being tripped in the hallway. I wish I couldn't remember someone throwing a pillowcase over my head and pushing me out the back door. I'm sorry I can recall falling down some stairs, rolling onto the grass, and smashing headfirst into what felt like a cement piling. Getting knocked out would have been much better!

I lay like a scared fetus with the pillowcase over

my head, afraid to move in case my attacker came after me again.

As I lay on the damp lawn, I noticed that the pillowcase smelled like gardenias. There are worse things than gardenias. I felt the wind on my bare feet.

Before I could decide whether to get up or to lie there forever, or at least until summer, someone pulled me up by the shoulders. Someone else pulled the case off my head. My head ached in the cold night air and I kept my eyes squeezed shut because it seemed like the safest thing to do.

Finally, after a long silence, I opened them and saw Ashton and Rick staring down at me.

"Hello there, my good man," said Ashton. He had a white scarf wrapped around his neck, like he just got off his yacht a few minutes before. Worried I was hallucinating, I pointed at it.

"You like my cravat?" he asked. "I've always thought one would suit me. Was I right or was I right?"

Okay, so maybe I wasn't hallucinating, but then realized that I couldn't remember my name. I looked around for the concrete piling, the one that had given me the concussion. It turned out to be a little apple tree. A sapling, really. So maybe my skull wasn't actually crushed, although it sure felt that way. I put my hands down on the wet grass and tried to push myself up, but pain made me sit back down. I groaned and put my head in my hands.

"Headache?" asked Ashton.

It hurt too much to nod. I was a man with no name! A man with no past and no future. A man with a wicked head injury.

I closed my eyes. When I opened them, a minute or maybe an hour later, Rick's face was stuck right in mine.

"Ashton, dude, do you think we should take him to the hospital? I think one of his pupils is bigger than the other."

"If we do, we better get rid of the evidence."

"What evidence?" I croaked. Thank God I still remembered how to speak!

"Of your interest in cross-dressing," said Ashton.

His words came at me from far away. They landed like lead slugs in my brain. Cross-dressing?

"Dude. You're wearing a woman's blouse," said Rick. "If it's supposed to be a disguise, it's the worst one I ever saw."

"Sherman, where are your shoes?" asked Ashton.

So that was my name. I felt a pang of disappointment.

"What happened?" I asked.

"You tell us."

"I was attacked. Someone tripped me and pulled that thing over my head. Then they shoved me out of the house."

"That's not good," said Ashton. He didn't sound nearly as upset as I would have liked.

"Where did you guys come from?" I asked.

"Rick snuck out of his house. And I got done with my oil painting tutorial early. Antoine passed out halfway through our still-life lesson."

"How did you find me?"

"We called Ben Kelsey's house, since we knew you were looking for the lacrosse party. We told his dad we were lacrosse players and we forgot where the barbecue was," said Rick. "He gave up the address no problem. I think he was hoping we'd help trash his ex-wife's place."

"We assumed you'd get into trouble trying to stake out the party by yourself," said Ashton.

"I wasn't in trouble," I said. "At least I wasn't until I got attacked. I came here with Vargo and Clarissa Kim. And Raquel George."

Rick turned to Ashton. "He's definitely got a concussion."

"I was surveilling Mac's for lacrosse players. And then these guys stole my bike, but Vargo and Clarissa saw and then they gave me a ride to the party. They had a blow-up doll named Guido. I don't know where he is now."

I stopped. I really did sound like a guy with severe head trauma.

"We'd better get out of here," I said.

Rick and Ashton pulled me to my feet.

"You planning to wear that blouse home?" asked Rick.

"Can one of you help me get this off? Don't rip it. It's Ben Kelsey's mom's."

Rick pulled on one sleeve and Ashton pulled on the other. They nearly dislocated my arms when they pulled the blouse over my head.

"Owww," I said.

Rick folded the blouse awkwardly and then jogged over and put it on the little porch landing beside the door.

"What about my shoes?" I said.

"If you think I'm going into a party full of drunk lacrosse players, you're even more brain-damaged than I thought," said Rick.

"Come on, Sherlock," said Ashton. "We'd better get out of here before you start singing show tunes."

I didn't take it personally, since he was wearing a cravat.

"Do you have any idea who attacked you?" asked Rick. I shook my head. All I knew was that whoever did it didn't seem very big.

THE TROUBLE WITH SEEDS

I don't think a person should focus on his failures all the time, but I couldn't help thinking how useless last night's surveillance was.

I got no evidence that the lacrosse team and Lester Broadside are the Defilers. I did nothing to help Anna. I haven't even seen Anna since the day she got defiled. Even the sort of make-out session with two of the hottest women at school couldn't make up for these facts. And anyway, that kiss wasn't real. They were messing with me. As far as the investigation went, I was just spinning my wheels. Or I would be spinning my wheels if those guys hadn't jacked my bike. Then I remembered that I'd dropped my shoes when I got jumped.

Great. Now I was going to have to wear the ones with holes in them.

I was so depressed that I didn't get up until after eleven the next day. I had just poured myself a bowl of cereal when my mom came wandering out of her bedroom. She wore wrinkly black satin pajamas. The shininess of the top reminded me of Mrs. Kelsey's blue blouse and I shuddered.

"I look that bad this morning?" she asked.

"No worse than usual," I said.

My mom stood in front of the open fridge and I began to get a bad feeling.

"Sherm. I've been thinking."

The bad feeling got worse.

"I've been working and dancing so much that I've been neglecting you."

I prayed that she wasn't going to say what I thought she was.

"No you haven't," I said, in a voice that was more like a squawk than I would have liked. My head still ached where I fell on it.

"Yes, I have. So to make up for it I'm going to make us a nice dinner."

My heart sank. I'd been counting on getting a proper meal tonight. Maybe some Chinese take-out. A grilled cheese and pickle. A nice bowl of cold cereal.

Every three to four months my mother has an attack of Bad Mother Guilt because she doesn't do a lot of the things that other mothers do, such as cook and clean, so she tries to make up for it by making complicated, the-opposite-of-tasty meals for the two of us.

Sometimes after her Sorry-I'm-Such-a-Bad-Mother meals, I have to take the next day off school because of stomach trouble. So I guess the meals do have their upside.

"It's okay, Mom," I said, trying to find an excuse. "I'm going to Fred's. He's helping me with some homework."

My mother frowned.

"It's for this project at school. A biology project," I said, getting warmed up.

She waved at the part of the shelf in the kitchen that holds her cookbooks—two cocktail recipe books and a copy of *Joy of Cooking,* which she won't use because it was a gift from Grandma. Whenever I suggest she look something up in it, such as how to boil an egg, she always says, "I take no joy in cooking." That makes two of us who take no joy in her cooking.

"Don't you want to come home to a nice hot meal?" she asked. "I was thinking of making tourtière!"

"Sure," I said, because I'm not totally heartless. "That sounds . . . uh, delicious." But I was worried because it also sounded *foreign*.

"It's French Canadian," she said, as though that was a good thing. "It's a meat pie! With spices. I heard someone being interviewed about it on CBC a few days ago." Instead of getting recipes from a book or the Internet or whatever, my mom gets them off the radio, Canadian Broadcasting Corporation. That means she never knows what anything's supposed to look like or how it's supposed to taste and has no idea about the ingredients.

French Canadian meat pie was a potential death sentence.

"Look, Mom. I really have to go. We've got,

like, a hundred plants to ID."

"Fine. Just don't forget dinner tonight. Maybe I should make Fred some?"

"Sure," I said, which wasn't very nice, considering Fred's never done anything to me.

Fred sat at the kitchen table. He was completely surrounded by little packets of seeds and stacks of gardening catalogs.

"Who's there?" he asked. "Is that Penelope Hobhouse come to put me out of my misery?"

"No, it's me, Sherm."

I slumped into a kitchen chair across from him.

"Sherman," said Fred, still not looking up. "Have I ever told you the problem with seeds?"

I shook my head.

"The trouble with seeds is that there are so many of them."

"I have to eat here today," I said.

"I hope you like seeds."

"Anything's better than French Canadian spiced meat pie."

His head finally popped up. Each of his eight

hairs went in a different direction.

"Tourtière is marvelous. Is that what your mother's making for dinner?"

I nodded.

"Don't look so forlorn. I should be so lucky as to have someone cook for me."

"She's going to bring you some," I said. "Then you'll change your mind. But that's not why I'm here."

"Romantic troubles again? Or more intrigue at school?" asked Fred. He's very psychic sometimes. I think it might be from spending so much time with plants.

Fred's not a tall man or a young man. He's got to be nearly forty. He moves like your average mostly bald middle-aged guy whose only physical activities are gardening and reading. The good thing about that is that I don't have to feel bad about my abs around Fred.

"I'll make us something for lunch and then we can consider how to proceed," said Fred.

I hoped he would make us a salad. I don't get enough greens at home because salad doesn't come in a can.

As if he was reading my mind, he pulled a bag of organic baby lettuce out of his fridge. He emptied it into a bowl and cut some sprigs from one of the pots of herbs he keeps in his windowsill kitchen garden and chopped them on his big wooden cutting board. I watched, trying not to look too impressed.

He spooned a bit of brown sugar into a small bowl, and added a splash of something red from a blue bottle. *Vinegar,* I thought to myself, *I bet that's vinegar!* Then he drizzled in some oil from a tall glass bottle that had white things floating in it.

"What's that?" I asked.

"Garlic-infused olive oil. My own garlic, in fact."

I was almost getting upset. Fred's cooking was making me *emotional.* Or maybe it was the leftover concussion.

He tossed the minced herbs into the bowl after he stirred the concoction around a bit more.

By this time, I was basically trying to hold back tears.

"So, Sherman, do I dare ask how things are going at that *Lord of the Flies* stage set you call a school? Has your young lady friend been thrust out of the social pack?"

"No, and I haven't figured out who's defiling people. It just happened to another girl. She was from my old school. It was pretty bad."

"Defiling? They actually call it defiling? How horrible. When a person runs afoul of the Vancouver Island Master Gardeners Society, things can certainly get ugly, but nothing like that."

I hadn't even mentioned how I'd had my bike jacked and been trapped in a blouse by the hottest girls in school *and* been assaulted by an anonymous attacker who threw a pillowcase over my head. Fred had no idea of the highs and lows of being an investigator. To be honest, I didn't want to get into it. I just wanted to take a break from everything and focus on lunch.

"I'll just broil a couple of chicken breasts and then we'll be ready," said Fred. He pulled a brown paper package out of his fridge, opened it, and took out two pieces of chicken and rinsed them under cold water. Then he patted them dry with paper towels and put them in a bowl. He sprinkled them with salt and rubbed it in. Then he used a little device to squeeze juice out of a lemon. He poured the lemon on the chicken and then ground fresh pepper onto everything.

"We'll just let them sit there for a few minutes before I pop them in the oven," he said, while he put two plates on the table. "That's free-range chicken. Local. Organic. Very nice."

I swear to God, I was practically bawling at this point.

"You okay, Sherman?" Fred asked, noticing my reaction. "This thing really has you wound up."

I said I was fine because I didn't know how to say it wasn't just what I'd been through lately. It was also seeing someone cook something I might want to eat. No wonder I can't get a girlfriend. Look at how I react to the sight of a salad and a piece of chicken! What is wrong with me?

CAN I OFFER YOU
SOME MEAT PIE?

I was just finishing the dishes when my mom showed up. She was carrying a big plastic container. It was filled with something brown and orange and steaming. As soon as Fred saw her, he straightened and brushed back his hairs.

"Hi," she said. "I hope I'm not interrupting Sherm's homework."

Fred shot me a look but didn't say anything.

"No," he said. "Certainly not. Come in. We just finished having a snack so Sherman could focus better on his, ah, homework."

"Oh," said my mother, her face falling. "I brought you some tourtière."

"My goodness! How thoughtful," said Fred, laying it on a little thick, considering the evil smell coming from the container, which didn't have a lid, because none of our plastic containers have lids.

My mom smiled. I think she even blushed.

I looked from her to Fred. What was going on here? Whatever it was, it was making my head hurt again.

I felt like telling Fred to get back to his seeds and my mom to get back to our house. I hadn't even had a chance to tell Fred any more about my investigation.

I walked over and took the container from her. The stuff looked even more disgusting up close.

"Thanks, Mom."

"Would you like a cup of coffee?" Fred asked my mother. "I made zucchini loaf last night." He turned to me. "Sherman, don't you think it's time we took a break?"

"But we just . . . and we haven't talked about . . . ah, never mind," I said. "I should go."

My mom and Fred got these matching disappointed looks on their faces.

"You guys can still have coffee," I said, but I didn't mean it.

"Absolutely!" said Fred.

I left before they could see my face.

As I came down Fred's front stairs the first thing I noticed was Lester's car parked across the street. Lester stared at me through the open window, his elbow resting on the window frame. He looked like James Dean.

"Hey, kid," he said as he pushed his hair off his forehead.

"Yeah?" I said. I was glad there was a whole street between us.

"Come over here."

I looked back at Fred's house. I hoped Fred and my mom weren't so busy shyly smiling at each other that they wouldn't hear my screams.

I crossed the street to Lester's car, looking each way about fourteen times. I stopped at least three feet away.

"If you stand in the road like that you're going to get run over," said Lester.

I moved another two inches toward him.

"So?" said Lester.

"So?" I said.

He drummed a finger on the white steering wheel. "What did you find out?"

I just looked at him.

"Jesus. Are you some kind of retard? Last night. I heard you were there."

Was there anyone the girls *didn't* tell?

"Did you find out about what might have happened to . . . Farrah? Or that other chick?"

How much could I trust him? Someone had thrown me out of the party with a pillowcase over my head. Could it have been him? I thought of the hands that pushed me. They hadn't felt that big. If Lester shoved me out of a house, I think I'd have flown a lot farther.

"Look, after what you said, I started to get suspicious. About the rest of the guys on the team. And that's not cool. They're my teammates, man. My buddies. You got me so paranoid, I didn't even bring Dini to the party last night. Just in case. Now she's mad at me."

Why was he telling me all this?

"I wouldn't want to think that I had anything to do with what happened to . . . her. Even like indirectly."

I thought for a second. I leaned on his car.

"Hands off the car, little dude."

I straightened.

I was trying to get my aching head around the fact that he was asking me what happened. He was asking me for help. It was a powerful feeling. It would have been even more powerful if I had any answers for him. I fought off a sudden strong urge to offer him meat pie.

"I'll look into it," I said, and started to walk away.

I was nearly across the street when he spoke again.

"When you talked to her, did she ask about me?"

"Who?"

He glanced down, then back up at me.

"You know, Farrah."

Her comments about finding out what he was made of popped into my head.

"No."

Disappointment was all over his face, but I didn't say anything. Instead I walked up the stairs to our house before he could ask any more questions. It was time to take a nap. Sometimes when a detective is stumped the best thing is to sleep on it. That's not a rule from *Learn To Be a P.I.* It's one I came up with on my own.

ON ANY GIVEN
BAD MOTHER SUNDAY

When I came out of my room after my nap I realized the house was really quiet and dark. No burlesque music playing in the living room. My mom's old sewing machine that she used to attach bits of feathers and sequins to inappropriate costumes was silent. The smell of cooking was starting to fade.

It wasn't like my mom to be away on a Bad Mother Sunday. I walked into the kitchen and looked out the window, across our brown lawn to the alley, where the bed of Mom's pickup truck stuck out of the garage.

Rubbing my eyes, I looked toward Fred's place. She couldn't still be over there. It'd been hours!

What could they be talking about that would take so long? They'd only be able to spend so much time talking about what a fine young man I am.

I tiptoed across our scraggly lawn in my socks and unlatched the old wooden gate that leads to our front lawn. Down our cracked, crumbling concrete steps to the sidewalk, up Fred's perfect concrete steps and into his flower-filled yard with its neatly cut grass. For some reason, instead of knocking on the door or going right in, I grabbed one of Fred's fancy tin gardening pails and carried it over to the kitchen window. I could hear voices inside. I had a sickening thought.

What if they were . . . you know? It hadn't even occurred to me that Fred would be capable, you know, given his obsession with plants and all. How could I have left them alone? I'd seen how his cooking had affected me. I could only imagine what would happen if he made a fresh salad for my mom, who probably hasn't eaten a full meal since before I was born!

I flipped the tin can upside down and silently placed it in the flower bed under the window. Then

I grabbed the sill and stepped up. I had just pulled myself to eye level with the window when my mother happened to glance out of it. She screamed. I screamed. She dropped the dish she'd been carrying and it shattered. I fell backward off the can.

A minute later she and Fred stood on his back porch.

"Hey," I said, still flat on my back beneath the window. "Whatchyouguys doing?"

They both shook their heads.

"Sherman," said Fred. "I think this detecting is getting out of hand."

"Detecting?" asked my mother.

ON THE RAMPAGE

My mother can be a bit dense. When we got home and I tried to explain to her that I'm investigating a few girls she kept asking why I was "spying" on them. I wanted to tell her about defiling, but I knew it would upset her, so I kept my explanation general. That meant that she didn't understand what I was saying.

"You're trying to find out why some girls in your school are unpopular? I'm sorry to break it to you, Sherm, but there are unpopular girls in every school. Unpopular boys, too."

"It's more than that."

"Really? How?"

"It's like, someone makes them unpopular. Intentionally."

"That's generally how it works. Sherman, honey, I know how much you like girls, but do you really believe you can stop them from getting jealous of one another? From picking on one another?"

When she put it like that my task seemed hopeless.

"Sherman, you have to stop spying on these girls. On any girls. And you definitely have to stop watching me. I told you, you don't have to worry about the men I date anymore."

She was referring to Gerard, her last boyfriend. He was a controlling jerk who didn't like me much, although he pretended to around her. He's the reason she doesn't date and has to express her sexuality through dance. Gerard was a bionic assweed.

"Fine," I said, because there was no point arguing. When she asked what happened to her bike, I decided it was best not to get too truthful. I also didn't mention the assault by an unknown suspect at the party. It is plain to me that she can't handle the truth.

"Someone stole it. At school," I told her.

"You rode my pink cruiser to school?"

"Yeah."

"Sherman, don't take this the wrong way, but I don't believe you. I know how concerned you are about appearing macho."

"Macho? No one's macho anymore, Mom."

"Fine. Manly, then."

"I'm not worried about that."

"I didn't say you were worried about *being* masculine. I said you were worried about *appearing* to be masculine. There's a difference. Do you need more men in your life than just Fred and your teachers? Is that what this is about?"

"Aw, Mom."

And just like that, she turned it all around so I didn't even get to ask her what she and Fred were doing alone together for four hours.

"I want you to promise to leave these girls alone. It sounds like they are having a rough enough time without you lurking around. You could get in trouble for that. You could get arrested!"

"Fine," I said. "But I wasn't lurking. I was . . . never mind."

"There's a girl out there for you. Why don't you

spend more time with Vanessa? I really like her. She'd make a wonderful dancer."

The thought of Vanessa in one of those burlesque outfits flashed through my mind again. I had to get rid of it quickly before I started to overheat. I just nodded at my mother because there's no point trying to talk to her when she goes on a rampage.

"Okay, I'll just put some meat pie in the microwave. You can eat and then do your homework and go to bed."

I am a crushed man. No wonder I worry about looking manly. I have to compensate for the neutering I get at home!

It will take more than my mother lecturing me and trying to poison me with meat pie to get me to cease and desist my investigation. As soon as I got into my room I pulled out my case log and reviewed everything. When the detectives in Vanessa's books get stumped during an investigation they usually go back to review the murder book. Those detectives are always saying things like "the answer is in the book." I seriously doubt the answers to this case are in my notes. I wish I had a few photos or pieces of actual evidence.

From where I stand, the problem is not enough evidence and too many suspects. If only I had access to a cool forensics department that could analyze hair and fingerprint samples and smoking-hot, older-woman, crime-scene investigators in tight clothes I could call to help. Of course, I wouldn't even have any hair or fingerprint samples to give a CSI.

Here's what I know: Someone, most likely the Defiler, snuck into cooking class and put that warning photo on our table. The Defiler must have been the one who attacked me at the lacrosse party. No one else had a motive. But I had no idea who'd snuck into cooking class. Mrs. Samuels didn't know the guy she kicked out, and I was so busy talking to Vanessa that I didn't notice anyone coming in or out.

I'd spent the entire lacrosse party in the closet and the girls didn't see anyone who seemed out of place. The only clue I had was that the hands that shoved me out the door and down the stairs were small but very strong. Could it have been a girl? A strong, small girl? As far as I know, only the Trophy Wives were at the party. Could they be connected to the defilings? I had a hard time believing they would defile anyone. They had no reason.

My head was starting to hurt from thinking too hard. I suddenly wanted to call Vanessa. I wanted to talk to a girl I could half understand so the world would start making sense again.

She answered on the second ring. She sounded cheerful.

"Hi, Sherm."

"Hey, Vanessa. I wanted to ask you something."

"Okay."

"Could the Defilers be girls?"

"Are you serious?"

I was offended by her tone. "Uh, yeah. Obviously."

"Sherman, I'd be surprised if the Defilers *weren't* girls."

"What? Why do you say that?"

"It's complicated. Guys are more in-your-face than girls. At least from what I've seen. Girls can be great but they can also be sneaky, underhanded bitches. More 'Sisterhood of the Traveling Snakes' than *Sisterhood of the Traveling Pants*. At least in my experience."

"Don't mint your words," I said.

"Mince. You're just so in love with every girl you see that you can't believe how brutal we can be."

"Do you worry about being so sinister at such a young age?"

"Cynical. And no, I'm just being realistic."

"Okay, let's say the Defilers are girls. They'd have a look in their eye, right? An edge to the voice? Something to show they are seriously messed up."

"I'd say the Defilers are definitely messed up. But don't count on being able to see it."

"Shit," I said.

"Sherm, I think what you're trying to do is amazing. I think it's noble of you to take this on. But maybe you should start by investigating something simple. Like how to stop drug trafficking in North America."

We hung up and the weird thing is that even though the conversation wasn't too positive or hopeful, I felt quite a bit better. Vanessa's so clear. I thought of her big brown eyes and my stomach went all mushy.

The phone was still in my hand when it rang again.

"Have you checked your email at school?" Rick asked.

"No. I've been busy investigating. Why?"

"I think you should look at it."

I cradled the phone to my shoulder and logged onto the Harewood Tech email program. The messages started downloading. The last one was entitled, Who's that Ho?

I clicked on it and a picture filled the screen. A picture of me. I was smiling all crazy, with my eyes half shut. I recognized Ben Kelsey's mother's closet. My upper body was squeezed into a shiny, blue blouse that was pulled up so you could see my stomach, which was not ripped. My feet were crammed into high heels.

I scrolled down. In the next photo I was kissing a dark-haired girl. Raquel!

The next photo showed two dark-haired girls kissing me. Raquel and Vargo. I looked drunk.

And happy. My hands were folded over my crotch, hiding my wood.

I stopped breathing. Pride and excitement passed by and left some weird shamelike fear feeling. I looked like a degenerate! What would Vanessa think? What would Clarissa's and Vargo's boyfriends think? It was just a game, but it didn't look like that in the photos.

I felt defiled.

"Who took those pictures?" asked Rick, his voice tinny through the receiver. I could barely hear him because of the blood sloshing around in my ears.

"I don't know," I said, a flat-out lie. Only one person could have taken that picture. Clarissa Kim. Strong, short, outdoorsy Clarissa Kim.

Maybe I was closer to finding the Defiler than I thought.

FINDING YOUR PLACE
IN THE MAN SLUT STORE

Now I know how Ron Jeremy feels. As one of the most famous male porn stars ever, he probably experienced many of the same things.

As soon as I walked into school it started.

"Hey, you cross-dressing sex freak."

"I like you better in heels. Made your ass look hoootttt."

"Dude! Two chicks at once. Sweeeeeet."

I nodded and smiled, like it had just been one of those wild weekends that happen to a guy sometimes. But I was nervous. The girls I was with in those pictures had boyfriends. Older, tough-ass boyfriends. I was a dead man.

Then there was Vanessa. I know we're just friends and all, but I couldn't face the disappointed look on her face.

There are two ways to handle a situation like this. One is to start explaining and making excuses all over the place and before you know it, everyone thinks you're even more of a dick. The second way is the James Bond method. Never explain or deny. It's the hard way, but as far as I'm concerned, the only way. So I toughed it out. People pointed at me, yelled stuff.

I powered through, giving the little smile and shrug, like it was no big thing.

The teasing was tough on Rick, though. He's not as sure of himself as I am. On the one hand, he was jealous that I'd made out with two fine older ladies. On the other, he didn't want to be seen with anyone who'd been photographed wearing a blouse and high heels.

Every time somebody made a comment, which happened about every ten seconds or so, he fell farther and farther behind me.

"Hey, dog!" said a ninth grader. "I'll take a piece

of that action. If I get me a pair of hooker heels, you think I can score a make-out session with a couple of Trophies?"

I pretended I didn't hear him.

"Doucheweed," said a girl I'd never seen before. Obviously the disapproving type.

I turned around to look for Rick and he'd fallen so far back I could barely see him.

I waited for him at the door to homeroom.

"Sherm, I don't know if I can handle this," he said, looking around nervously.

"Fine. You can cut me loose until they get tired of it. But then you're going to owe me big-time for your disloyalty."

"You sure it's okay?"

"Yeah. You'll be back. It's not like you have any other friends."

"Thanks, man." Rick looked down the hallway and noticed two of the cuter girls in our class headed for us. They looked at me, then giggled and whispered something to each other. Rick disappeared like a puff of smoke in a strong wind.

When the girls walked past me they smiled in

this "we know what you did last weekend, you dirty slut dog" kind of way. I'm a man of steel, so I wiggled my eyebrows and smiled back.

That made them laugh, and I laughed right along with them, but my heart wasn't in it. How could Clarissa have betrayed me like this? I thought we were friends, but she set me up. Maybe they all set me up: Clarissa, Vargo, and Raquel. I just couldn't figure out why.

I made it through to lunch, and when the bell rang, I went looking for the Trophy Wives. I started at the *Harewood Watcher*. I figured if Vargo's boyfriend, Pete, was in a motorcycle accident, he probably wouldn't be at school editing the paper. So you can imagine my surprise when I walked in to see that he was the only guy in the room. He sat in front of a computer. There wasn't a scratch on him that I could see.

"You okay?" I asked.

He swiveled around in his chair.

"I've been getting that question a lot lately," he said.

"I heard you had an accident. On your scooter."

"That was just some jerk's idea of a joke. Scared the hell out of Vargo."

"So it wasn't true?"

Pete shook his head.

I waited for him to say something about the picture of me kissing his girlfriend. He was the editor of the paper. He knew everything that happened at school, from the student council's plans to get Coke to be our corporate sponsor to who tried to make their own sex tape. I knew he'd seen the email. Everyone had.

He looked at me, Mr. Mild. No trace of homicidal rage on his face.

"So," I said.

"So."

"Do you know where Vargo is?" I asked.

I hoped that wouldn't be the last straw, the one that sent him into a jealous rage in which he smashed my head into a computer monitor and then did terrible things to me with a keyboard. That's what I'd want to do if I saw a picture of my girlfriend making it with another guy.

"Try the cafeteria. She wants them to offer a

vegan menu. Or she might be hanging out down at the edge of the field."

To get to Vargo I would either have to go into the cafeteria, which is basically the lion's den of teasing, or cross the no-go zone of superjock sadists on the sports field. Two equally crap choices.

"Thanks."

"No problem."

I cleared my throat.

"About that picture," I said. "Of me and Vargo . . ."

He looked at me, all quietly intelligent and calm.

"It wasn't anything, you know, serious."

He smiled. I was starting to see why Vargo went out with him, I mean besides the fact that he's tall and handsome and smart. If I spent much more time with him I was going to get a man-crush on him, just from how chilled out he was.

"She told me what happened."

"She did?"

He nodded and leaned forward. "If you find out anything about what's going on in this school, you come see me, okay?" Then he turned back to his monitor.

This guy was probably one of the coolest guys I've ever met. I mean, he didn't even mention the cross-dressing.

All the Goths stared at me as I walked up. They looked undead and unhappy, which I think is the point. Some of the girls were quite attractive, in a scary sort of way. If my mom didn't work almost that exact look herself, I could see myself getting quite attracted to Goth girls. As it is, the whole thing hits too close to home. A guy shouldn't start being attracted to girls who look like his mom until he's in his twenties.

Vargo stared at me right along with the rest of them until I got real close and then, finally, she smiled and her face lit up.

"Sherman," she said.

I hadn't expected her to sound so friendly. I had to remind myself that she was possibly a dirty double-crosser.

"Vargo," I said, trying to keep my voice cold steel to let her know I was mad.

The Goths glanced at each other. They all seemed to have extremely large eyes. I think it's a side effect from wearing so much black eyeliner.

Now that I'd found her, I didn't know what to say. So I stood there like a bonehead. One of the Goths giggled and whispered something to another one.

"What?" I asked.

"You look different in runners," said a tall, thin boy wearing a tall, thin hat, who spoke in a high, thin lispy voice.

"We all like you better in heels," hissed the girl beside him. She held her cigarette between two long, black fingernails. Any minute her trailing black sleeve with the lace trim was going to catch fire.

"*You guys* are making fun of my clothes?" I asked, genuinely surprised.

I turned to Vargo.

"I thought we were friends," I said. "Why'd you set me up? Get Clarissa to take my picture. When I was . . . you know . . . in a compromising situation. You left me in the closet. I got jumped when I tried to leave."

The amused look faded off Vargo's face. "Slow

down. You got beaten up?"

I nodded.

"Sherman, I had nothing to do with that. You were playing your little dress-up game with Raquel. I gave you a quick kiss because you were such a good sport. Then Clarissa and I got that call. Someone set *us* up. I was the one who had to explain that picture to Pete."

"So who took the photo? Who posted it to the school email system?"

The Goths looked from me to Vargo like we were giving a bondage demonstration on the Life Network.

Vargo looked thoughtful. Unlike me, she's probably pretty good at thinking.

She didn't answer my questions. Instead she said, "Raquel didn't come back to get you?"

I shook my head.

"And someone beat you up?"

"Yeah. When I tried to leave. Someone tripped me. Put a pillowcase over my head. Shoved me out the door. I fell down the stairs. I almost got a concussion."

I could see that Vargo was trying not to smile.

"But you're okay? No permanent damage?"

"No, but it was close."

"Who do you think jumped you? The guys from the lacrosse team?"

"No. It felt like just one person." I didn't tell her that it felt like one *small* person.

"Sherman, it wasn't me. I was at the hospital making an ass of myself, thinking that Pete was there."

"What about Clarissa?"

"She was with me."

"But she took those pictures of me," I said.

"I guess she must have. There was no one else in the closet. I haven't talked to her since that night. But even if she took them I don't think she would post them. Clarissa smokes a lot of weed, Sherman. She doesn't have that kind of drive and initiative."

"None of this makes any sense," I said. "Someone's out to get me, and it had to be someone who knew I was in that closet. Someone who knows I'm after the Defilers."

Vargo just stared at me.

A HELPING HAND HUG

For the first time since I got to Harewood, I was dreading cooking class. I hadn't seen Vanessa and I didn't know what she was going to say about those pictures. She probably thought I was a loser perv-hound. Maybe she was right. Mrs. Samuels was expecting me to hand in my final menu for the big project which, due to my brain injury and emotional trauma, I hadn't finished on the weekend. For those reasons I didn't exactly dance my way into the home ec room. I kept my head down and went straight for our unit. I didn't even glance in Vanessa's direction.

"Yo, Sherm, we've got carrot cake today!" said Rick, sounding fairly happy for once.

I ignored him while I made notes about what I

should do next. First thing, I had to speak to all the defiled girls and reinterview Farrah. Find out if they knew of any reason Clarissa might be after them. I would have to get Anna to come out of her house to talk to me. Then there were the other two girls Farrah told me about. I'd lost the piece of paper with their names on it. For an investigator, I was pretty disorganized.

"Sherman?"

Mrs. Samuels stood in our entryway. "Is that your menu you're working on there? As you know, it's due at the end of class. I'm hoping it's going to be a centerpiece in our Cooking Nine Cookbook!"

"Uh, sorry, Mrs. Samuels. I had some, you know, family issues this weekend."

Mrs. Samuels's face went all serious and sad. "Oh no," she said. "I'm so sorry to hear that, Sherman."

"Yeah." I nodded and tried to look like I was from a deeply dysfunctional family and pretty troubled, which wasn't hard.

"Did this family trouble occur before or after you had your little photo session this weekend?"

I dropped my pen on the floor.

"Sherman, I know that the chef personality is

one that likes to live close to the edge. I know what goes on in kitchens after closing time. Many a tremendous young talent has been wasted by letting the fun and games take precedence over the food."

"Yes, ma'am."

"I want that menu by Wednesday. Or you won't be getting into the Cafeteria Program until eleventh grade. Nor will you have a place in the Cooking Nine Cookbook."

I nodded, and she smoothed her apron and walked away.

I was so rattled from that conversation that I accidentally looked toward Vanessa's cubicle, the way a drowning person looks at a lifeboat. She was staring right at me. Her eyebrows were practically touching her hairline, but she didn't look mad.

Might as well get this over with. I took a deep breath and stood.

"Dude," said Rick. "Situation critical on the carrot cake! Needing some assistance!"

"Aren't you supposed to be keeping away from me? You know, for your reputation?" I said.

"I can hang out with you in here. You're my partner, so I don't have a choice. Plus, a lot of people think you're the man, now that you've made it with two Trophy Wives. Even if you were wearing heels and a blouse at the time. I think we can be friends again."

"Grate the carrots," I said. "And if Mrs. S. comes around, tell her I'm borrowing a measuring cup."

"You gonna talk to Vanessa?"

I nodded and he made a good-luck face, the one where he screws up his mouth and bugs out his eyes.

I ran my fingers through my hair, which didn't do anything for it one way or another, and walked over to Vanessa's unit.

Edna snorted, which made her sound like a bear in a garbage dump. I shrugged at her and looked at Vanessa. She was wearing her apron the way only Vanessa can. I tried to get my nerves under control. Vanessa and I had been friends since we were infants, practically. Why was I getting so wigged out around her now?

"Hey," I said.

She was measuring spices into a bowl. Cinnamon. Allspice. Nutmeg. The smells of Christmas. Of family. Of comfort.

"How's it going?" I asked.

She looked up. "Oh hi, Sherm. You here to rescue us from carrot cake?"

"Just checking in."

"Very nice of you," said Vanessa. She stirred a fork around in the bowl to mix the flour with the spices. "The real question is, how are *you*?"

"Okay," I said.

"You've been busy," she said. Not accusing. Just stating a fact.

"I can explain that."

"I'm sure you can."

She didn't sound mad, which kind of worried me.

"It was all part of my investigation."

"Oh?"

She still didn't sound upset. Didn't she care that I was photographed making out with two hot older women?

"I was staking out the lacrosse party. Because I heard some guys on the team might be involved. . . ." I lowered my voice so Grumpy Guts Edna couldn't hear. "In Anna's, you know, D-listing."

"And you somehow ended up in women's clothes making out with a pair of Trophy Wives?"

"It wasn't like that. The girls got a little bored."

For the first time I could see something change in Vanessa's face. She did care.

"Bored," she said. "Right."

"Seriously. They were just messing around. It didn't mean anything."

"It means something now. Everyone in school has seen those photos. Rick said you got beat up right after those pictures were taken. It's like *you're* the one getting defiled."

"I can't get defiled. I'm a guy."

"Don't kid yourself. And even if you can't get formally defiled, one of those Trophy girls' boyfriends could happen to you." She stirred the spices a bit harder. "I'm starting to be sorry I put you onto this whole thing."

"I'm going to figure it out. I just need some evidence."

She reached up and poked me lightly in the chest with her fork. It sent a shot of electricity up my back. "Do you need any help?" she asked.

I shook my head. All I really wanted from her was a hug, but I wasn't about to tell her that.

"I can't believe you haven't given up," she said. Then she put down the fork and held my hand for a second. Her hand was warm and soft. It was like she was giving me a hand hug! It was incredible.

"Sherm," she said. "You really are such an idiot." And just like that, the day went from being one of the worst to one of the best. I realized that if Vanessa ever kissed me instead of poking me with a fork and touching my hand, I'd probably die of happiness.

I was still grinning like a fool when I walked back into our kitchenette. Rick had scraped his knuckles across the grater, leaving blood all over the shredded carrots.

"I hope you're smiling because you want to make the cream cheese icing," he said.

I just kept smiling as I reached for the mixing bowl.

LIKE TIMMY, ONLY OLDER
AND MORE OF A LOSER

"Ed?" I asked as I cracked open the bathroom door.

No answer.

Great. We had to play this game again. The only reason I was putting myself through this was I needed the names of the other two defiled girls that Farrah had given to me before. I figured it would be easier to get them from Ed than to track down Farrah.

I walked all the way in and bent over to look for Ed's huge white runners in the stall.

"Ed, it's me. Sherman Mack. From detention?"

Behind me, the bathroom door opened and I froze.

"Look who we have here," said a deep voice.

I turned and looked up, way up, to see Ben Kelsey blocking the light. Tal Manhas, Raquel's boyfriend, stood right behind him. Tal had to stoop to get through the doorway.

This wasn't good.

"Hi," I said. "Ed's not here, but I can take a message if you want."

"Pervert," said Ben Kelsey.

"Ed's a little different, but I don't think he's an actual pervert," I said, trying to keep things light.

"You snuck into my house, into my mom's closet, you little freak," said Ben Kelsey, who was tall and dark, a bit like King Kong.

"You made out with my girlfriend," said Tal Manhas, who may be a scholar and an elite athlete, but also seems to have a dark and violent side, judging by the look on his face.

"You put on my mom's clothes," said Ben Kelsey, in a voice that was surprised and upset, like it hurt him to get the words out.

"So you recognized the location? That's interesting, if you think about it."

They came closer, a wall of threat closing in on me.

"You trying to be funny?" said Tal Manhas.

Ben Kelsey dropped my shoes on my feet.

"You left these in my house."

"Who writes their name in their shoes?" asked Tal.

I decided not to tell them how Rick and I have the same shoes and we wrote our names in them so we wouldn't get confused.

"You're just lucky I didn't catch you in my mom's closet. I would have beat your ass," said Ben.

"Never too late," said Tal.

With that they grabbed me and slammed me into a wall. Ben slapped me across the side of my face.

"You got any more funny remarks?" asked Ben before he hit me again, like he was trying to wake me up from a faint. His hand was so big, it was like being slapped with a ham.

I waited for the ringing in my ear to get quieter, then said, "You better hit the other side, too. It's starting to get jealous."

"You want to see jealous?" said Tal Manhas, reaching down and grabbing the waistband of my shorts. He pantsed me so hard I screamed.

They started turning me around and around by the shoulders while they did something with my arms. At first I didn't know what they were doing. Then I realized they were taping my arms! And my legs. I tried to kick, but one of them held me tight. I tried to yell, but there was a ham across my mouth and all I could do was make dying mouse noises.

Next thing I knew I was hanging upside down. I was sure they were going to dunk me in the toilet. What a horrible, horrible way to die. My squeaking got faster.

They didn't put me in the toilet but instead plunged me headfirst into a black hole filled with wet paper that smelled bad and felt worse. The garbage bin. I waited to be dropped.

"Careful you don't break his perverted little pencil neck," said Ben, grunting a bit from the effort of holding me. I was happy he was keeping my safety in mind.

"He's a heavy little turd," said Tal.

They swung me right side up again and smashed me feet-first into the big black garbage bin. With my arms taped to my sides and my legs taped together, I felt like Timmy down the well, only older and more of a loser. I wished I had a collie dog to rescue me.

I tried to look extremely dangerous, like all hell would break loose if they let me free, but I was still dizzy from being spun around and held upside down, and I don't think it really came across.

Ben and Tal turned to leave.

"Hey—" I said. I knew as soon as I said it I'd made a mistake. I should have kept my mouth shut.

Ben Kelsey ripped off another piece of tape and slapped it across my mouth.

"Stay out of my mother's closet," he said.

"Don't ever look at Raquel again," said Tal.

Then they were gone.

DESTINATION
SINK AND BEYOND

After you get your ass kicked multiple times in a few days, you realize that you can get used to anything. Seriously. I was barely even upset after being pummeled by Ben and Tal. A lot of the detectives in Vanessa's books don't even feel like they've worked a full day unless they've been shot at or blown up. As an investigator, it's my job to stay cool in all situations. So that's what I did.

Using tiny little jumping motions, I tried to inch the garbage can toward the sink. I'm not sure what I thought the sink was going to do for me, but it's always good to have goals.

I was so focused on Destination Sink that I barely

even noticed when someone walked into the washroom.

"Sherman Mack, what on earth are you wearing this time?"

I jumped around to see Raquel George in the doorway. She looked fantastic, her long hair shining and her nose ring picking up the light, standing there in the boys' washroom.

"Mmfff," I said from beneath the tape.

"You're really into this dressing-up thing, aren't you?" she said. Her teeth were brilliant white and made a nice contrast with her frosty pink lip gloss.

"Mmfff," I said.

She walked farther into the washroom and looked around.

"Ed's not here?"

I shook my head.

"It's not like him to leave the office during business hours."

I nodded. It was all I could do.

Raquel walked toward me, smiling. I couldn't help flinching when she pulled a blade out of her bag. I was so busy staring at the silver blade that I nearly fainted when she leaned forward and ripped the tape off my mouth with her free hand.

"Ow!" I said.

"Sorry about your mustache."

She was just being polite. I don't have any facial hair.

I looked from her perfect, painted face to the silver blade.

"It's a nail file, Sherman. A girl never knows when she's going to run into bound and helpless boys who need to be cut loose. Turn around."

I hopped around inside the bin so I was facing the wall and tried to think of what to say. The nail file wasn't a switchblade, exactly, but it was disturbingly similar to a shiv, which is what prisoners use to stab each other. I decided this wasn't the ideal time to confront her about abandoning me in a closet only two nights before.

"Hold still," she said. "Or I'm going to poke you."

Here's the sick thing. I was trying to keep still, but the way she was messing around with the tape was making me, well, let's just say that Ben and Tal should have tied something else down, too. I'm sad to say that there doesn't seem to be anything that *doesn't* turn me on.

I tried to edge up to the side of the bin so she wouldn't notice, and for the first time I was glad for all the soggy paper around me, and disappointed in myself for getting a boner over the most random things.

"You need to stop moving or I'm going to stab you." To show me she was serious, she pricked my shoulder with the nail file.

Great, I thought, *another* fetish. I'm going to spend the rest of my life wanting girls to poke me in the shoulder with sharp objects.

Finally, she finished sawing through the tape.

"Are your feet taped, too?" she asked.

"I'll get them later," I said. No way was I coming out of that garbage can until everything had calmed down, you know, down there.

She slipped her nail file back into her purse.

"Look, I'm sorry about leaving you at the party. Something came up."

I tried to give her a you're-not-fooling-me look. It was hard since I was standing in a garbage can.

She didn't notice, anyway. No one ever notices my looks.

"And I'm sorry that picture of you got posted. I swear I didn't mean for that to happen. It's just that Clarissa sent it to me, just for our private files, you know. And one of my friends saw it and thought it was funny. She sent it around before I could stop her. No hard feelings?"

I nodded. A small one.

"I'm glad I could help you with this little situation, at least. I hope we're even now. Have you seen Ed?"

I shook my head. I couldn't think of a single thing to say. It was basically a boner-got-your-tongue situation.

"Damn. I'm supposed to interview him to get some pointers on the pro-legalization argument. If you see him, tell him I stopped by."

I watched her walk out. Her clean perfume stayed behind. If I closed my eyes it was like standing in a garden beside a laundry exhaust instead of in a garbage can filled with wet paper towels.

THE CLOTHES
MAKE THE DEFILED

I was at my locker early the next morning when I heard somebody near me take a sharp breath. I turned, and a wave of people swiveled to look at something, at someone, coming down the hallway.

She walked with her head held high, taking hard, short steps. It was Anna, and she looked more defiant than defiled.

As she came closer, my jaw dropped. She definitely wasn't going for the low-profile, beat-down and defiled look, unless by "low" you meant her black vest. It was cut to expose maximum cleavage. Her tight red skirt was dangerously short. She had on high, black boots that didn't look like they fit very well. Her hair was wild.

Anger made her cheeks stand out red against her white skin. She looked like she'd lost weight. Whatever she was doing hiding away in her house after the defiling, it wasn't eating.

I realized she shouldn't be doing this. The Defiled were supposed to fade away or at least stay on the fringes. But here was Anna all up in everyone's faces, as on-display as it was possible to get.

At first no one said anything. But then the murmurs started, quiet at first, getting louder.

"Sssslut."

"Look at that. Who does she think she is?"

"Dares to show her face."

"I can smell her from here."

My heart started to thud painfully in my chest. Anna had almost reached my locker but her steps slowed. I took a quick look to my left. Ahead of her, a knot of faceless people blocked the way.

I wanted to throw a coat over Anna's head, the way they do for criminals, and get her out of there. She stood across from me. Her nose flared as she breathed in and out, almost panting. I thought of a spooked horse in a burning barn.

I didn't see where the balled up pieces of paper came from. Anna flinched away. Then an eraser bounced off her cheek and her head jerked back like she'd been slapped. Then she was being pelted. Pens, erasers, food, gobs of spit that landed in her hair.

I launched myself at her but somebody beat me to it. Dini, in her paint-stained black shirt, her face distorted with rage and tears, stood in front of Anna, holding her arms wide, as though she wanted to grab the whole crowd and shake them.

"Stop!" she yelled. "Please, stop."

I looked around for a teacher but there were none in sight. It all happened so fast.

For a long second it looked like it worked. That she'd called them off. But then a crunched-up lunch bag hit Dini on the side of the head and the stream of missiles started again. I saw a notebook hit Anna in the back and she staggered into Dini. By the time I reached them, objects big and small, sharp and soft, were bouncing off me. I kept my arms around the girls and started pushing them toward the back door. Someone kicked at my leg and I nearly went down. The hot breath of the crowd was in my hair. I was shoved into the girls when a punch landed in my ribs.

I kept going, grunting as people punched and kicked us on our way out the door.

ON A STICK

The three of us stood outside after the door closed behind us. We were all crying a bit. Part of it was relief to be outside, breathing air that wasn't filled with hate; part of it was just plain crying.

Dini rubbed the back of her wrist against her eyes and took a deep raggedy breath.

She looked at Anna.

"It's okay," she said. "They didn't follow us out."

Anna's makeup was smeared down her cheeks. The red splotch on her cheeks was gone and her face was gray. She stared at the ground. Dini made a move as though to touch her, and Anna jerked away. She took two quick steps to the side and threw up in some sad old shrubs planted against the back of the school.

I couldn't seem to get my eyes to stop leaking.

The three of us stood there. Anna facing the bushes. Dini and I watching her.

The back door flew open and we all jumped, ready to run.

"What's going on?" demanded Coach Little.

Dini and I looked at each other. If I looked even half as messed up as she did, we were in trouble.

"She's sick," said Dini, nodding at Anna. She did look sick. And drunk. Like she just downed a bottle of Peach Schnapps to help with a wicked case of the flu. She also looked like she'd lost her entire family in a fiery accident about ten minutes before. She looked destroyed.

I glanced at Coach Little. For the first time ever, I was glad to see him.

I nodded. "Yeah. She's not feeling well."

"What happened in there?" he asked. "I thought I saw a scuffle."

I wanted to tell him. This whole scene was way beyond my ability to describe. People went mob on us. They tried to kill Anna. They tried to kill Dini and me when we got in the way. This wasn't a Mack Daddy investigation anymore. This was total craziness on a stick.

"Nothing." Anna's voice sounded like it was being dragged over glass. "Nothing happened. I just need to go home."

That voice. It sounded like the beginning of a scream that would never stop. Me, Dini, and Coach Little each took a step toward her.

"I'm fine," she said, louder this time. She was staring at me and shaking her head ever so slightly. "I just need to call home."

"Well, come on into the office, then," said Coach Little. His voice was actually soft. He stepped back up into the doorway and held open the door for her.

When she walked past me, she muttered something.

"You two. Get to class," said Coach Little. Then he ushered Anna into the hallway.

That left me and Dini standing on the back stairs.

"What did she say?" asked Dini.

"She told us not to say anything," I said. "She said it would just make it worse."

* * *

I barely got through social studies and had just finished smiling at Vanessa before handing in my
menu for the Cooking Nine term project, which I
finally finished last night at around three in the
morning, when a kid came into our classroom and
handed a note to Mrs. Samuels.

"Sherman, you're wanted in the office," said
Mrs. Samuels.

I swore under my breath. I was still feeling a
little shaky after my run-in with the mob. I thought
things like that happened only to Joan of Arc and
brave African-American kids who integrated schools
during the civil rights movement. I never thought it
could happen to me. I couldn't believe that people
in my own school could go so apeshit. It turned my
stomach. It really did.

I hadn't even told Rick what happened. He'd
been trying to find out ever since I got into class,
but I didn't know what to say to him. I'm fairly sure
I had a touch of post-traumatic stress. I could only
imagine how Anna felt.

At the office, I was told to sit on a chair and

wait. I watched the elderly secretary with big hair answer the phone and reapply her lipstick about twelve times.

Finally, Coach Little opened the door to one of the offices.

"Mack," he said.

I got up and went in.

The sign on the office door said MR. VENDI, ASSISTANT VICE PRINCIPAL. I've never seen him. I heard he's been on stress leave since the middle of last year due to an incident with his pants. At some point it might be worth investigating what exactly happened to Mr. Venti and his pants, but for now I've got my hands full.

Coach Little sat down behind the desk. He looked out of place in his gray track suit.

"You going to tell me what really happened this morning?" he asked.

Coach Little may be homely and have yellowed, pushed-in teeth, but he's not stupid. He knew there was more going on than one girl with an upset stomach.

"What did Anna say?" I asked.

"I'm asking the questions here," said Coach Little, whose authoritarianism is never far below the surface.

"She got sick," I said.

"Look, Mack. There's something rotten going on in this school and I want to know what it is."

I looked right into his beady, bloodshot-from-too-much-exertion-with-the-medicine-ball eyes.

Could this man handle the truth?

"I agree with you, sir," I said.

The corners of his mouth went down.

"What?"

"There is something rotten going on in this school."

We stared at each other for a while.

"You going to tell me what it is?" he asked. He waited. I didn't reply.

"Do you have anything to do with it?" he asked.

I shook my head.

"Does this have anything to do with it?" He shoved a piece of paper toward me. It took me a few seconds to realize what I was seeing.

It was a photo of Vanessa. With a small D

marked underneath. My vision went black at the sides and I felt my fingers dig into the padded vinyl arms of the chair.

"Where did you get this?" I asked, my voice barely working.

"I found it in one of the washrooms about ten minutes ago."

There had to be some mistake.

"I have to go," I said, trying to keep my voice under control.

"This conversation isn't over," he said.

But I was on my feet and running for the door.

35

D-LISTED

Vanessa looked at me like I was crazy when I ran back into the home ec room and grabbed her arm.

"Are you okay?" I asked.

"What?"

Her beautiful face was cheerful. Undefiled. Undestroyed.

I looked around us. Listened for the voices. Nothing. People hadn't heard.

I saw Edna walk into the room. There was something wrong with the way she was staring at Vanessa. Something vicious in her expression. She knew.

"Vanessa, we've got to go," I said.

"Sherman, we're making cupcakes. I've been waiting all term for this. This is going to be the highlight of my entire school year."

"I'm serious," I said. "Something's happened."

Rick walked up behind me.

"Sherm," he said. "I found something in the washroom."

His face was white. He held a piece of paper in his hand. A photograph.

"We've got to get you out of here," I said. "Before the break."

Vanessa noticed the piece of paper in Rick's hand.

"What's that?" she asked.

Rick and I didn't say anything. How do you tell someone that her life is about to turn into a nightmare?

"Come on," I said. "We'll walk you home, but we've got to go now."

She took a deep breath and blew it out. Then she untied her apron strings.

"Sherman?" said Mrs. Samuels.

I squeezed my eyes shut so I wouldn't yell in frustration.

"Yes, Ma'am?"

She held up my menu.

"This is wonderful. Simply wonderful. I want you to put on this dinner on Friday. If you need extra time in the kitchen after school to practice, you just let me know. Whatever you need, Sherman. This shows real . . ." Her voice trailed off but she made a small fist-pumping gesture of triumph.

"Thanks, Ma'am," I said. And even with everything going to pieces around me, I was happy.

"This is going to be a center piece in the Cooking Nine Cookbook. I knew you wouldn't let me down," she said.

Then she went bustling off to the next unit, and Rick and Vanessa and I rushed out of the room. Edna stood off to the side, and as we passed she whispered something foul.

We pretended we didn't hear.

When we got into the hallway we all looked from side to side. Like robbers.

Vanessa looked again at the piece of paper Rick still clutched in his hand. "Is that what I think it is?" she asked.

Rick stared at the floor.

I nodded.

"Shizzz," she whispered. "This isn't good."

"Come on," I said. "Get your coat and we'll go out the back way." Rick and I were wearing our coats, like we always do to make ourselves appear larger. The back was safer than trying to sneak her out the front way, in full view of the office.

The halls were deserted. No one had seen the photographs yet. With the one Coach Little took and the one Rick found, there would be no photos in two of the busiest bathrooms, for a little while at least.

Rick hesitated at the back door.

"I should try to take down the rest," he said, holding up the piece of paper in his hand.

"Are you sure?"

He nodded.

"We can slow it down, anyway," he said.

"Be careful," I told him. He nodded again, then patted Vanessa on the shoulder like he was afraid she'd break before he walked quickly back down the hallway in his shuffling way. Mr. Unlikely hero.

Vanessa and I slipped out the back door, then ran across the parking lot and onto the street. We didn't stop running until we were two blocks away.

* * *

Vanessa lives in one of those Old City houses that's been fixed up so it looks even nicer than a new house. It's a green two-story with white trim around the windows and doors and a white, wooden porch. It looks like a house with good manners—the kind of good manners you get when people care about you. It reminded me of Vanessa.

We stood on the sidewalk in front of her stairs and neither of us really knew where to look or what to say. Vanessa had on a knee-length coat. When she looked at me her face was pale. I found myself staring at her face like I was trying to memorize it before she went invisible, like the rest of the Defiled.

"Sherman, could you please stop staring like that?" she said.

"I'm going to fix this," I said.

She blinked. Her eyes were the prettiest brown in the world.

"How?" she asked.

"I'm going to find out who's doing it."

She closed her eyes and I could see the soft pink veins in her eyelids. When she opened them again, tears welled in the corners.

"I'm really scared," she said.

I thought about what happened to Anna this morning. What happened to me and Dini when we tried to get in the way.

"We'll fix it," I said. "I've got an idea."

"I think Edna saw the photo," she said. "She gave me this awful look when we were leaving." A big tear fell down her cheek.

"Edna's got mad cow," I said. "She looks at everyone like that."

Vanessa laughed and a few more tears fell. I wanted to brush them off her cheeks, so I did.

She stopped laughing and looked at me. Her eyes were huge.

"You'll hear from me soon," I said. "Until you do, don't go out. Right now, none of this is real. It's not real until they catch you. I have a plan."

She nodded. I turned and walked away.

As terrible as it was, it may also have been my finest moment.

TO-DO LIST

That thing I told Vanessa about having a plan? Not strictly true. What I had was more like a collection of thoughts. A to-do list.

1. Investigate what the Defiled have in common. The addition of Vanessa made things even more confusing, but there had to be something.
2. Flush out the Defiler(s).

When I got back to school it was lunch hour. Feeling like I had a target on my back, I headed for my locker. My plan was to pick up my backpack and leave for the rest of the day. I knew I was probably going to get in trouble for running out on

Vendi and Coach Little, but some things are more important than school. I had to find Farrah and track down the rest of the Defiled.

I headed for the Alternate, which is a portable trailer parked on the edge of the school grounds. The Alternate is where the kids who are too smart or too antiauthoritarian or just plain too alternative take their classes. The Alternate is sort of like protective custody for the hard-core weirdos, the ones who can't survive in the general school population.

To get there, I had to walk past the bleachers. Sure enough, there was Dini, alone on the top step with her square black notepad on her lap and a charcoal pencil in her fingers. I couldn't see any marks on her after the brawl this morning. In fact, she looked fine. Better than fine. Excellent, even.

"You okay?" she asked.

I nodded. "You?"

"So that's what you worried might happen to me?" she asked. "What happened to that girl this morning?"

I nodded again. I remembered Lester telling me he was going to give me a thumping if he caught me hanging around her again. I'd taken so many thumpings recently, I couldn't work up any concern.

"I knew people got defiled. I just never thought about what that meant," she said.

"I'm sorry," I said, because that's what I always seem to end up saying to girls.

"That was the worst thing I've ever seen," she said. "Do you really think Lester has something to do with it?"

I considered for a second. "Not really. But it happened to his last girlfriend."

"Brutal," said Dini.

"I have to go," I said. "I'm looking for someone."

"Wouldn't happen to be a girl, would it?" asked Dini. She was looking past me at someone headed our way. It was Farrah. I checked out Dini. Did she know Farrah was a Defiled? Did she know Farrah was Lester's ex?

She knew.

"Hi," I said to Farrah as she got closer. I forced myself not to check to see if a mob was about to come rushing out of nowhere and kick our asses.

"I heard about this morning," said Farrah. "That

girl stuck her neck out. Drew attention to herself. You can't do that." She sounded mad and looked surprisingly unconcerned. Farrah stood straight and her hair was pulled off her face. Her skin was clear. I looked at her purse. She'd even glued the rhinestones back onto her bird.

"I need the names of those other girls again," I said. "I have to talk to them."

"Is it true about your friend?" she asked. "That she just got D-listed, too?"

I could feel Dini glance at me.

I nodded.

"Punishment. For you. Your friend, she doesn't fit the profile," said Farrah.

"There's a profile?"

"I think so."

Farrah turned to Dini. "You should be careful," she said. "You're more the type."

"The type?" Dini asked.

"Bad girls making a play for good boys. Losers getting above themselves."

Farrah stared at Dini. "Loners who start dating Mr. Popularity."

Farrah reached into her purse and pulled out

another piece of paper. She wrote on it and handed it to me.

I looked at the names. Linnea Lehane and Jayne Manklow.

"Do you know where I can find these girls?"

"You're too late for Linnea," said Farrah. "She was put on the list two years ago. No one's seen her for at least a year. I heard she moved."

"What about Jayne?"

"You're probably too late for her, too."

"She moved away?"

"She tried to kill herself."

Beside me I heard Dini take a sharp breath.

"What happened?" I asked.

"She took some pills a few weeks ago. With some drinks. Accidentally on purpose. I don't know if she's still in the hospital or not."

I looked more closely at Farrah and realized she was holding back tears. If there's one thing that kills me, it's when girls cry.

I didn't know what to say and she didn't give me a chance to figure it out. With her back as straight as an arrow, Farrah turned and walked away from us, across the empty playing fields. I thought of Lester telling me to tell her hello for him.

The silence between Dini and me was deafening.

"That was Farrah," I said finally.

"I know who it was," said Dini. "She's the one who used to go out with Lester."

I looked at her.

"He told me some of it. It's time for you to tell me the rest."

SOCIAL ENGINEERING

When I got home that day I couldn't think too well, because I was hungry and still had a bit of post-traumatic stress disorder.

I thought about the interesting fact that not one person I've talked to is down with defiling, and I've talked to a lot of people. In fact, half the school seems to know that I'm investigating defiling. Does anyone support defiling, or is it only a faceless mob thing?

Those of us who disapprove are like a resistance movement or something. Like that guy in Mexico, Chaz Guevara. That's as far as I got in my thinking because I was so hungry that my brain just shut off.

It was time to visit Fred.

"Sherman, how are you?" he said, looking up from his laptop.

"Pretty good," I said, but I tried to look kind of skinny around the face so he'd offer me some food.

"How goes the investigation?"

I rubbed my stomach to show how starving I was before I answered.

"It's getting kind of intense."

I looked toward his fridge. I wished I had X-ray vision so I could see inside it.

He finally took the hint.

"Sherman, before we get into it, perhaps you should go in the fridge and get the cheese and some juice. There are some crackers in the top cupboard."

I pulled out a block of some smokey-smelling cheese and a glass jug full of juice with a thick layer of froth on top.

"Fresh-squeezed pineapple pear juice," he said. "I think you'll like it."

After I brought all the stuff over to the table, he

asked me to go get a cutting board and some plates. Fred sliced an apple and the cheese and laid some crackers around them on a big plate. Then he poured us each a big glass of juice. At Fred's house, all the plates match. He's civilized like that. Fred may not get out much but he definitely knows how to live.

I tried not to eat like a starving dog, but it was hard. When it was all gone, I carried the dirty plates over to the counter.

"A man needs decent food in his stomach if he wants to think deeply," said Fred.

I couldn't have said it better myself.

"So what's going on?" asked Fred.

I laid the whole case out for him, except the parts I didn't want him to know, like how I got caught wearing ladies' clothes and stuff. I told him that lots of people know about the investigation and that one of the Defiled tried to off herself. I told him about getting assaulted in the hallway, about Vanessa getting D-listed.

"Good lord, that's terrible," he said. "Are you sure you don't want to report all this to the authorities?"

"What are they going to do about it? It's the students. The teachers can't make us stop."

"I think it's more of a 'them' than an 'us.' After all, *you* don't go along with it," Fred pointed out.

"Yeah, but me and my friends . . ." I didn't quite know how to finish that sentence. Were different? Better?

"You're a very fair young man," said Fred. "And I suspect your friends are the same."

I could feel my face go red. I felt glad Fred was my mentor.

"What do you want to do about it?" he asked.

"I want to stop it. I want the defiled girls to stop feeling bad."

"You need to bring these girls into the fold, Sherman. If you do that, you might flush out the people behind this campaign."

The minute he said it I had a total brain wave. It was an idea so radical it even made me a bit breathless. If nothing else, my plan would show who was serious about not liking defiling and who was more of a faceless mob type.

"Fred, you're a genius!" I said.

"I'm glad you think so. Confused, but glad," he said.

A FEW TOO MANY COWS

Making up invitations is a pain in the ass. First you've got to put the address and the date on there and all the little details, like what time dinner will be served. Then you've got to make photocopies and hand them out to all the people you want to invite and avoid all the people you don't want. It's a lot of work, especially when you're nervous of some of the people you're inviting.

My friends were easy. When Rick called, I picked up the phone and said, "I'm putting on a dinner for cooking class on Friday night. You're coming."

"What?"

"My term project, fool. So I can get into the Cafeteria Program next year. Remember? I have to put on a dinner party. I get to invite people and cook for them. Like one of those people on the Food Network."

"This isn't going to be like the rest of your cooking, is it? You know, where you get distracted and leave me to do everything?"

"No, man. I would never do that. But you are going to have to help."

"That's what I was afraid of," he said. "And what about Vanessa? What are we going to do? Shouldn't we be focusing on her instead of some cooking party?"

I ignored him.

"Leave that to me," I said.

Next I called Ashton. I told him he could wear his cravat if he felt like it. I knew he'd bring a touch of class to the whole party.

After those two, the invitations got harder.

Rick stayed right behind me when I walked up to Trophy Wife Territory the next morning.

Vargo and Clarissa and Raquel stood around Clarissa's scooter. Guido was tied on the back. He had on a Speedo.

"Hello, ladies," I said. "I'm having this little

thing here at the school on Friday evening. A bit of a get-together. I'd like you to come."

The girls glanced from one another to me. Then they cracked up.

"A thing?" said Vargo.

"A dinner party," I replied. I was trying to sound like one of those guys from the beer commercials who is used to having hotties around him at all times.

"A dinner party?" said Clarissa, like she was speaking some foreign language.

"Yeah. I'm making dinner for some people. It's part of my term project for Cooking Nine. So I can get into the Cafeteria Program a year early."

"And you're inviting us?" said Raquel, as though the idea was unbelievable.

"I know how much you fine ladies support academic achievement and culture."

That cracked them up again.

"You're really something, you know that?" said Vargo, and for a second I thought she was going to hug me again. "Does this have anything to do with the case?"

"No, just good food. Good friends," I said.

They hadn't said no yet. I had to lock this down before they realized that it would be bizarre for a trio of Trophy Wives to go to a ninth grader's dinner party.

"Seven o'clock Friday. Come ready to eat," I said. Then I walked away without looking back.

When I returned to Rick, who was waiting at the invisible dividing line that separates Trophy Territory from where the commoners stand, his mouth hung open. He was impressed, I could tell.

"Did you just invite *all three* of them?"

I shrugged, like it was no big thing.

"You are the man," he said.

I sort of had to agree.

I couldn't find Lester alone, so I had to go up to him when he was sitting in the cafeteria with some guys from the lacrosse team, including the dreaded doucheweed Ben Kelsey. I pretended I didn't notice the other guys. Lucky for me, my pants are pretty baggy, so they couldn't see my knees shaking.

I thought about inviting the whole lacrosse

team, since they were all sort of suspects, but it was too dangerous. Plus, I couldn't afford to feed all of them and they probably wouldn't come. One lacrosse player would have to be enough.

"Here." I handed Lester the piece of paper.

"What's this?" he asked.

"Invite," I said, in my toughest voice.

"To what?"

"Prolly his little birfday party," said Ben Kelsey, with his mouth full of food.

"You gonna have wittle pony wides at your party?" asked another player.

"Just read it," I said to Lester, ignoring his friends.

Then I cruised away, cool as a cucumber. When I got back to Rick, who'd stayed out of sight near the door, I thought he was going to bow down before me.

You know that poem that has the line "and miles to go before I sleep"? That's how it felt giving out those invitations.

I was nearly as nervous giving Farrah hers as I

had been giving Lester his. To get to her, I had to walk over to the Alternate again. Farrah sat outside the portable with her back against a tree. She was reading some book with the word *Dunces* in the title. She had on tall lace-up boots with fur trim at the top. They weren't the boots of a defiled girl. They were defiant boots like Anna's outfit. I felt nervous for her and proud of her all at the same time.

"Hey," I said. "I've got something for you."

"What's this?" asked Farrah.

"A dinner invitation."

"For me? Is there going to be anyone else there?"

I knew what she was asking.

"It'll be fine," I said. "You'll be fine."

She bit her bottom lip, then seemed to realize what she was doing and stopped. She gave me a long look, pulled her ponytail over her shoulder, slipped my invitation between the pages of her book, and kept reading.

I left an invitation in Anna's mailbox, even though I was pretty sure she wouldn't come. Then I got Jayne Manklow's address out of the phone book.

There was a Manklow's Automotive and then a C. Manklow, who lived a few blocks south of our place, and about a block and a half from the big white and red Hells Angels clubhouse.

I was just going to slip an invitation through the mail slot, more as a gesture than anything else, but the second I stepped on the lawn, the front door of the Manklows' house practically flew open.

"Hello?" demanded a lady in a pink sweatsuit.

"Uh, hi," I said.

"Are you here about Jayne?" asked the lady. She didn't sound too upset or anything. She sounded sort of excited. Maybe mental illness ran in Jayne's family, the way liking lingerie does in ours.

"Sort of. Yeah. I mean, I have something for her. Is she home?" I prayed silently that she wasn't.

"Oh, isn't that sweet! Jayne's not home, but you must come in."

"That's okay. I'll just leave this for her." I tried to hand the lady the invitation, but she wouldn't take it.

"Absolutely not! You must come in. It's starting to drizzle! I wondered when Jayne's school chums would start dropping by."

School chums?

I stopped on the top step and tried again to hand her the invitation, but she wouldn't take it. She kept the door open, leaving me no choice but to walk inside.

"Can I get you anything? A drink? A snack?"

"No, I'm good. Just wanted to drop this off."

I looked around for a table or something to put the invitation on, but the entryway was empty and very clean. The whole house smelled like those cleansers my mom doesn't use because she says they cause cancer, although the truth is that she doesn't clean at all.

"I insist!" said the lady, her voice getting a bit screamy, like a machine in the metalworking shop. "Just take off your shoes before you come in."

I took off my shoes. Things never seem to go right for me when I take off my shoes.

As soon as my runners were off, the lady grabbed them and put them away in a closet. I felt like a prisoner. Next she'd be asking for my belt.

"Come in and sit down."

I followed her into a living room with light blue

walls. The carpet was light blue and I could see the vacuum marks in it. The velvety-looking couch was light blue with a black-and-gray pattern that looked like smudge marks but probably wasn't supposed to. I felt worse for Jayne Manklow by the minute.

Jayne's mom looked from me to the couch a couple of times. She was sizing me up.

"Actually," she said, "let's sit in the kitchen."

The kitchen had light blue linoleum on the floor. The blue was just different enough from the blue in the living room to be irritating. The kitchen had a cow theme. A strong one. The containers lining the counters were ceramic cows. There were cow salt-and-pepper shakers by the stove, black-and-white cowhide-patterned tea towels, and framed pictures of cows on the walls. I was starting to think that maybe living here was what sent poor old Jayne over the edge. Maybe getting defiled was just the last straw.

I sat down on a chair with a cow-print seat and Jayne's mother poured me some milk in a glass with a picture of a heifer on it.

Then she got me a cookie. One cookie. A lame-looking one, from a no-name cookie bag. She put it on a cow plate.

"Here you go," she said. She stood over me while I ate the cookie and drank the milk. The house was so clean I felt like I had to take small bites.

The dried-out cookie tasted funny. Unnatural. Like she'd used some of her cleaning products on it.

Finally, I got the last dry, little chemical-tasting crumb down and finished the milk. Mrs. Manklow hadn't said one word. She'd just stared. Poor Jayne Manklow. I couldn't imagine being defiled at school and then coming home to this. The psych ward at the hospital would probably be a relief after this house.

"Okay, I'll just leave this here," I said, putting the invitation on the table. "I should probably get home. I've got lots of homework to do. At home."

"Oh, isn't that lovely," said Jayne Manklow's fairly crazy mom. "I will pass along your regards to Jayne!"

"Okay, then," I said. I got up from the table and she stood in front of me. Blocking my way.

"What was your name again, dear?"

"Sherman. Sherman Mack."

Her skin was bright and shiny but covered with

a lot of fine wrinkles.

"I'm so glad you stopped by."

I wanted to shove her out of the way, but that would have been rude.

"If you see Dee, please tell him to stop by the hospital. I know Jayne would love to see him. They were always such good chums."

"Dee?"

Her voice turned into a whisper. "Dee Snider. Jayne's young man. Her first real beau. Such a lovely boy. He got her away from that bad crowd." Mrs. Manklow lowered her voice. "She'd been doing drugs," she whispered. Then, like the sun coming out from behind a small cloud, her face brightened. "Dee gave me my cow clock," she said, waving at a cow-shaped clock on the wall. "Of course, I haven't seen him in quite some time. I think he and Jayne are just friends now. It really was so nice of you to stop by."

I waited for her to get my shoes out of lockup and practically ran out of there when she opened the door.

Dee Snider. Where had I heard that name before?

A SMALL-TO-MEDIUM-SIZED GET-TOGETHER

Feeling like a very serious detective, I checked out Harewood Tech yearbooks online to find out more about Dee Snider. He was in twelfth grade. There were no pictures of him in any of the three yearbooks I looked at. Just a blank silhouette with the words "Have you seen this man?" underneath.

I checked three years' worth of team pictures for the lacrosse team, but there was no Dee Snider listed in any of the team pictures. I made a mental note to ask Farrah if she'd ever heard of a Dee Snider. Then I thought of Mrs. Manklow telling me that Jayne used to do drugs. Was that relevant? It was another thing to ask Farrah. Was she also a current or former druggie?

When I finished making notes in my report log, I walked down to Tim Hortons and got myself a large coffee with triple triple and came home. I needed strength for what I had to do next.

I dialed Vanessa's number.

Her dad answered.

"Vanessa's not feeling well," he told me in his fancy English accent.

"Yes, sir. I know, but I just wanted to pass along a message from one of our teachers."

"I'll give her the message, if you like," he said.

"Dad?" Vanessa came on the line. "It's okay. I'm awake."

"Are you sure?"

"I'm fine."

"Keep it short. You really haven't been looking well." There was a click as he hung up.

"How are you?" I asked.

"Excellent," she said, being all dry and Vanessa.

"Just hang in a while longer. I need you to come to school Friday night."

"After what you said happened to Anna? Are you crazy?"

"You have to trust me. I want you to come to my dinner."

"Oh, God," she said.

"It's okay. I have a plan."

"Does the plan involve me being attacked by a psychotic mob?"

That hurt my feelings and I told her so.

"I'm sorry, Sherm. But my nerves are on edge."

"Just come to the dinner. It's at seven o' clock. You'll be perfectly safe. I'll make sure of it."

She made a slightly rude noise.

"Actually, maybe you could come at around six. I might need some help."

Another rude noise.

"It'll take your mind off things. What have you been doing, anyway?"

"I'm supposed to be too sick to watch TV, so I've been reading a book by this guy called Michael Connelly."

"Any good?" I asked.

"The best. He's got this detective called Hieronymous Bosch. He reminds me a bit of you."

"So he's pretty cool, then?"

"He used to be a tunnel rat in 'Nam."

Vanessa is always telling me the detectives in her books remind her of me. It's how she gets me to read the books. I'm a sucker for flattery.

"Sounds like we have a lot in common," I said.

"Oh, you do. You should read it when I'm done."

After a few more words, Vanessa hung up. I was just thinking about how she might be the coolest girl ever when my mother yelled from downstairs.

"Sherm! Could you come in here, please?"

I didn't answer right away because I was still thinking, and I prefer to do one thing at a time.

"Sherrrman!"

My mom doesn't give up easily.

I walked downstairs and into the kitchen. I tried to look as innocent as possible. It wasn't hard because basically, I am pretty innocent.

"What is this?" she asked, holding up my shopping list for the dinner party, which I'd left out for her to find.

"A list."

"What kind of list?"

"A list for the dinner party," I explained.

"Dinner party?" she said.

"You know, it's where people get together and eat. Usually happens in the last part of the day."

"Sherman Mack, don't get smart with me. Who are you having over that requires"—she stopped to look at the list—"two pounds of Belgian chocolate?"

"It's a school project," I said. "So I can get into the Cafeteria Program a year early. I told you about it a while ago."

"You didn't mention any two pounds of chocolate."

"I need a good mark. They don't fast-track just anyone into Cafeteria."

She shook her head. "Does your grandfather know you're trying to become a cafeteria worker? God, I'll never hear the end of it."

"Mrs. Samuels said the dinner party project is about good friends and good food."

"Good food?" said my mother. "You're in ninth grade. Aren't you supposed to like crap?"

I didn't dignify that with an answer.

"Just how many people are you planning to invite?"

I shrugged. The details would just make her worry. I don't think my mother has ever had a dinner party. She usually brings energy bars to potlucks.

"How many, Sherman?"

"I don't know. Around ten. Or twelve. It depends."

"That seems like a lot to ask. Honey, you know I love you and admire you tremendously. But putting on a dinner party for ten or twelve people is serious business. I'm not sure I could do it."

I tried not to let her see what I thought about that last statement.

"It's okay, Mom. I've been training. And I'm putting on the dinner at school. The teacher will be there. She'll be supervising."

Her face relaxed a bit.

"Well, that's good, I guess. But this is still a lot of food. . . ." She looked at my shopping list. "How are you going to afford all this?"

I cleared my throat. "I thought maybe you could help. Since it's for school."

"This cooking class is going to bankrupt me. I really don't know where you developed this obsession with food. Life was so much simpler when all we ate was toast."

"Will you take me shopping Thursday night?" I asked.

She nodded.

"Thanks, Mom. You're the best," I said. And the funny thing is, I really meant it.

I waited until she left for work, then I made sure I had all my surveillance supplies, including my jar, and headed out. By the time I got to Vanessa's, it was raining, but her yard has quite a few good hiding spots. I found one that kept me mostly dry. I watched over her house until one o'clock, just before my mom was due to get home from work, and I didn't fall asleep once.

40

IT'S HARD TO CATCH PERPS WHEN YOU'RE COOKING

My mom dropped off all the groceries we bought at three-twenty on Friday. That was a proud moment. My mom's old truck, shaking and rattling, pulled up and parked in front of the Trophy Wife Territory. Mom was dressed for rehearsal. She had on this black throw trimmed with feathers over the top of her costume. The sight of her froze everyone around us. When she started lifting bags of groceries out of the passenger side, I edged up and tried to speak to her very quietly.

"Uh, Mom? Could you maybe pull up around to the side of the school?"

She handed me two bags of groceries. "I'm late

for practice. The girls are going to have my hide if I'm late again today."

I took the white plastic bags and set them on the sidewalk, off to the side of Trophy Territory.

"It'll just take a minute," I said. "This stretch of pavement, it's, well, it's kind of reserved."

My mother straightened and looked around. With her hair wrapped in a black silk scarf that was tied into little points that stuck up on top, and dressed all in black, she looked like she was starring in a musical about bats.

"For what? All the limos lined up to take kids to their palatial estates over on Bruce Ave?"

I gave up and hustled the groceries off to the side.

She'd just handed me the last two bags when I heard a girl's voice say, "I looove your outfit."

I turned to see Vargo standing behind me. She was staring at my mom like she'd just spotted her favorite celebrity.

"Your makeup is fantastic!" she added.

My mother smiled, like she'd been expecting the compliment.

"Are you Sherman's sister?" asked Vargo.

My mom's smile became even more pleased.

"Charmer," she said. "I'm his mother."

The two of them shook hands. I shuddered when I noticed that they both wore black nail polish.

After they finished signing up for the girls-who-wear-black mutual admiration club, my mom turned to me.

"Okay, Sherm. I'll be at rehearsal, but I'm not working tonight, so you call when you're ready to come home. Or if you get into trouble with all this"—she looked at the pile of white bulging plastic grocery bags like she couldn't quite think what to call it—"food."

"Sure, Mom. Thanks."

She walked around behind the truck and got in. It took a few tries, but she finally got it started. It backfired loudly as she pulled away. One of the stoner guys in the parking lot dropped to the ground like he'd been shot. I noticed that she'd used two of her scarves to tie the bumper on.

"Your mom is really amazing," said Vargo as we watched the truck turn the corner. "She's so young!"

I couldn't argue with that.

"So dinner's at seven, right?"

I nodded.

"We'll be there," said Vargo. "Clarissa, especially, is looking forward to it. She has an appetite like three truckers."

I wondered whether Raquel had told Tal about the dinner. I hoped not. I didn't want to end up in another garbage can while I was trying to make dinner.

I started to panic about fifteen minutes after I unloaded the groceries. I wasn't ready to put on a dinner party! I hardly ever even made it through a whole recipe in class, never mind all the recipes I was supposed to be making for this dinner.

Rick was sitting on the floor, reading, a sure sign that he was stressed to the max.

I tried a little deep breathing, but that just made me dizzy.

How could I have invited all these people who could basically be divided into lions and lambs to the same party? Someone was going to get killed, if not by each other, then by my food.

A few minutes later, Mrs. Samuels stopped by and asked how everything was going. I guess she noticed I hadn't done anything except put all the groceries onto the counter. When she reminded me that three hours isn't as much time as I might think, I tried to give her a confident, Mack Daddy–type smile to ease her fears.

She asked who was doing the table. I didn't know what she meant, so I said Rick was.

"Are you going to make it beautiful?" she asked him. "Because you know that presentation is part of the mark."

"*I'm* not trying to get into the Cafeteria Program," whined Rick, looking up from his book.

"Yes, but part of what Sherm is demonstrating tonight is that he can get others to work for him."

"I'll work for him as soon as I finish this chapter," said Rick.

Mrs. Samuels left looking not quite as cheery as she normally does.

I slumped at the kitchen table. Regular people with regular moms would call home right about now and get some help. But my mom was off doing erotic dances with her troupe and telling dirty jokes. Plus, it wouldn't be smart to let her near the food. Then I had an idea. I sat up straight.

"Fred!" I nearly yelled.

Rick ignored me.

I ran for the phone in the office.

I left Fred a message on his voice mail telling him I had an emergency. I also told him that if he was able to help, he'd have to do it on the down low, since I'm not supposed to get much help, except from useless people like Rick.

For some reason, asking for assistance, even if no one came, made me calm down a bit. I washed the asparagus and put it in a pot with some water. Then I started the soup. The soup recipe was pretty fancy and Mrs. Samuels told me I had to substitute something non-alcoholic for the champagne, so I wasn't sure how well it was going to work out. I just hoped that white wine vinegar is similar to champagne.

As for the main course, which was chicken, I was feeling pretty good about it. Mrs. Samuels said cooking is all about preparation, so I put all the packages of chicken in a pile beside the stove.

My dinner had an aphrodisiac theme, although I didn't tell Mrs. Samuels that. I found the menu on a romance website with a feature on what it called sexual superfoods. The asparagus, Brie, and oyster soup were supposed to get people in the mood to get along. I thought that was important, since I'm going to mix people who wouldn't normally be caught dead together.

According to the website, garlic chicken Parmesan and spaghetti are supposed to make people feel intimate. And the vanilla ice cream, strawberries, and chocolate sauce will finish things off on a happy, possibly sexy, note.

I laid all my recipes on the counter and asked Rick when he was going to set the table.

"In a minute," he snapped. Rick is going to have a hard time if he ever gets a job in a real restaurant because not every chef will be as easygoing as me.

The good news was that Ashton and Bennett showed up almost two hours early.

"You want some help with the table?" asked Ashton.

"For real? I'd owe you big time."

"Not at all, my good man," said Ashton. He was wearing his cravat. Bennett went to sit on the floor in the corner with Rick, and Ashton asked for directions to the art and theater rooms. I didn't ask why. It's best not to when you're dealing with someone like Ashton.

With Ashton in charge of décor, I turned back to the menu. I soon learned that wine vinegar is not a good substitute for champagne. Also, I'd started the soup too soon and the oysters turned into little rubber balls. Deformed, gray rubber balls. The cream curdled and for some reason the Brie cheese all floated around on top. The whole thing looked like a mess and smelled worse.

When Mrs. Samuels came around to see how I was doing, I slammed the lid onto the soup and said I couldn't take it off because it was rising.

"The soup?" she asked.

"Yeah. It's one of those really fluffy ones."

She frowned a little bit. This dinner of mine was really challenging her cheery nature. In fact, it was kind of boning my happiness, too.

People would be showing up in less than two hours and I'd already lost what was supposed to be my sexiest dish. It was time to check on the tables.

Fortunately all those art classes Ashton has taken really paid off. He lined up two long tables in the middle of the hallway outside the cooking room and covered them with paper from these huge rolls they keep in the art room. Then he put all these paperclip sculptures down the middle and a lot of little cups filled with regular pencils, colored pencils and pens, and candles that he took from the school's emergency kits, which he really wasn't supposed to touch. He put twelve chairs around the tables. As a sort of joke, he set up a separate table for Mrs. Samuels. He made it look good, too, by covering it with an old velvet curtain he found in the drama room. He put Mrs. Samuels's table and chair on a few risers so she could look out over our tables.

When the janitor showed up he said the tables were a fire hazard, but Mrs. Samuels came along right behind him and got him calmed down. She told me that no other student had served their final dinner in the hallway and that it was a very innovative approach that really pushed the envelope. She said some of the most popular restaurants were housed in unusual settings. But she couldn't give me any examples.

As soon as she left again, I started on the chicken. I was just rolling the first piece around in the garlic butter and Parmesan cheese and bread-crumbs mixtures when something occurred to me. There was no way I'd be able to surveil the dinner party if it was in another room! I dropped the piece of chicken on a plate and ran out into the hallway. Ashton came out of the drama room wearing one of those velvet Shakespeare-era hats. It looked good with his cravat.

"Dude, you have to move the table or I won't be able to watch!"

"My good man, I'm a designer. Not a laborer. I don't do furniture. Sounds like a job for our herni-ated friend."

He meant Rick.

I raced back into the kitchen and told Rick he had to move the tables into the home ec room

ASAP. He complained a bit, but I pointed out that if he'd set the table the first time like I asked, he wouldn't be in this situation. If cooking and detecting don't work out for me, I may become a teacher or a naggy mother when I get older.

That emergency solved, I took a minute to assess the situation. I had one piece of chicken ready to cook. People would be arriving in an hour and a half. No wonder that English chef on TV swears so much. Cooking is even more stressful than detecting.

Fred showed up at 5:35. The first thing he said was, "Take a deep breath. No one ever got through a dinner without breathing."

I've noticed that most adults are obsessed with basic bodily functions.

"I'm screwed," I said.

"Just tell me what you need me to do."

"Everything. It's all a mess . . . the soup . . . everything." Then I thought of Mrs. Samuels. "But I'm not supposed to get help from an adult. I'm supposed to be in charge."

"I see."

He pulled the recipe printouts off the counter.

"Brie and oyster champagne soup?" he said.

"It's in here," I said, pointing to a pot.

He lifted the lid, then put it back on really fast. He looked shaken.

"Okay, what else have you got?"

"Chicken Parmesan. Pasta puttanesca. Vanilla ice cream with strawberries and chocolate sauce."

"Good. We can work with that. First, I want you to take the soup and throw it down the toilet. Actually throw it down a few toilets just to be safe. I don't think one toilet can handle it."

"But I'm trying to make food that will help people get along."

"If you serve that soup a war will probably break out at the table. People may be trampled in the rush to get away from the soup. I'll make you a soup."

"Can you throw out the soup?" I asked Bennett, who was still sitting in the corner reading.

He nodded, face very serious.

"Don't let Mrs. Samuels catch you," I said.

He got up, grabbed the huge pot in both hands, and moved toward the door.

"Like a shadow!" I yelled after him. "Nearly invisible."

"A shadow with a mysterious foul smell trailing after him," said Fred. "So you're making twelve pieces of chicken Parmesan?"

"And I'm serving asparagus."

"Very nice," he said.

"Yeah. It's already started. I've been cooking it for about"—I looked at the clock above the door—"twenty-five minutes."

Fred blinked. Then he stopped breathing. When he started again, he said, "When the kid gets back, send him to the Dumpster with your asparagus."

"But it's expensive!"

"If asparagus is fresh it should be steamed for two minutes. If it's old, eight minutes. I'll bring you some carrots."

"Oh, man," I said. "I'm going to fail the Last Supper."

"The Last Supper?"

"That's what I've called my project for the Cooking Nine Cookbook. Mine is going to be the featured menu."

"You might want to rethink the name."

Fred started moving pots and pans around on

the stove like a chess player. Or an iron chef.

"You need to break down the tasks. Finish preparing the chicken. Make your pasta sauce and put the water on to boil. I'll be back."

I froze. "Where are you going?"

"I'm going to get you a soup and some carrots. All you have to do is dip that chicken like you were doing and put the ingredients for the sauce into the pan and start a pot of water boiling. Get a helper. I'll be back in"—he looked at his watch—"thirty minutes. Tops. Keep an eye on this window."

Fred half walked half ran out the door, nearly crashing into Rick and Ashton as they carried the long table into the cooking room. I went back to dipping my chicken, calmer now that I knew Fred wouldn't let us starve.

Lester and Dini showed up at 5:45. You'd think I'd have been excited to see Dini but I am over her in that way. To make things worse, Dini and Lester didn't seem to be getting along. He stood near the door like he was waiting for something. Maybe he was waiting for someone to rescue him from a ninth grader's dinner party.

Rick kept asking Bennett and Ashton if they could hear ringing noises. He said he felt itchy all over, like he was having an allergic reaction to something I was cooking.

Dini asked him if he wanted her to take a look and I thought he was going to have a stroke. Even Ashton jumped. He hadn't forgotten how hard she tackled him that time he was pretending to be injured.

Then Dini asked me if she could help. I said she could cut up some apples and oranges and melon and pineapple that I bought to serve as an appetizer and between courses.

When I finished dipping the chicken, I made the mistake of looking at Lester. The look he gave me jammed up my nerves so bad, I couldn't keep opening cans of tomatoes for the pasta and I had to go into the bathroom to calm down.

When I came out, the place was crawling with Trophy Wives! Without their boyfriends!

They were talking to Ashton and Rick and making everyone feel happy. Their perfume even overpowered the last little bit of overcooked oyster-vinegar smell.

They even got Dini to laugh a couple of times, but I noticed that she laughed the way people do when they're thinking of something else. Maybe she was thinking about Lester, who was still staring at the door.

In between chopping garlic and olives and onions, I kept a superclose eye on the Trophies. If one of them was the Defiler, she was definitely going to react when she saw the other guests.

You know, I think girls may be the key to a successful dinner party.

I didn't hear Fred when he knocked on the window. Rick saw him and sort of screamed. High-pitched. Like a girl.

I turned and saw Fred standing by the window. A fraction of a second later he disappeared.

"Stop yelling," I said to Rick. "It's Fred. With some food."

"Jeez, man, you have to warn me if there might be sudden noises."

I turned to the rest of the room. Lester and Dini and the Trophy Wives were all staring at the now-empty window. I was glad Mrs. Samuels wasn't on one of her reconnaissance missions.

"Nothing to see here, nothing to see," I said. "Just an old family friend come to pass along his regards."

I hustled over to the window.

Fred wasn't alone. My mother was crouched beside him under the window.

"Why aren't you at rehearsal?" I asked her.

"I'm done. How's it going?"

"Okay, I guess. What are you doing here?"

"I went to visit Fred. He was making your soup. He invited me to come say hello."

I frowned at Fred, even though I knew I shouldn't because he'd made me soup and everything.

"Here," he said, holding up a big silver pot.

I looked from him to my mom once more. She carried another pot.

"Yeah," I said. Then I realized that I sounded sort of ungrateful. "Thanks," I added.

He gestured at the window. "The pot's not going to fit through the gap."

"Come around to the back door," I said.

"I'll wait here," said my mom, after she passed me the smaller pot, which turned out to be full of uncooked carrots in a metal steamer, through the open window.

I put her pot on the stove and went to meet Fred at the back door.

He handed me the pot. "Cauliflower soup with pesto," he said. "I just defrosted it. It's better than it sounds."

"What are you doing with my mom?" I asked.

"She was excited about your dinner. We're friends."

"Are you dating now?"

My stomach was upset. Like I had the flu or something.

"I like your mom, Sherm. But nothing's going to happen that you aren't comfortable with. Maybe she just needs a friend."

"She's bad with men," I said. "She's got bad taste."

Fred nodded seriously. "So she tells me."

For some reason that made me feel better. Lighter.

"Thanks for the soup."

"It's my pleasure. If you need anything else,

call. Your mom and I will be having coffee at my place."

I looked at him.

"Just remember that your support team is nearby."

The soup was so good I almost forgave Fred for potentially wanting to bag my mom. Okay, that's not true. But he came through large on the soup! It was like velvet. The man may have only eight hairs but he can handle a cauliflower!

Encouraged by the soup I got to work on frying the chicken, and put the pasta on to boil. The puttanesca sauce was good, stinky from all the garlic and olives and everything, but that's the point. Everyone was hanging around the cooking room, chatting and eating pieces of fruit off the fruit tray. The fruit tray was like art. Every piece was cut into a cool shape. I saw Dini explaining to Ashton how she turned the orange peels into swans. Ashton had better make sure Lester didn't see him making time with Dini or Lester would strangle him with his own cravat. But Lester was still waiting at the door and not noticing anything.

By 7:06 I was freaking because my key guests weren't here. The dinner party wouldn't do anything but feed people if I couldn't get the right people to come. I yelled at everyone to sit down, and Mrs. Samuels came over and told me that a dinner party was not a military operation. She could have fooled me.

Rick and Bennett helped me put the soup on the table. I put a sprinkle of parsley on each bowl as it went, which is the kind of thing that can bring a guy's mark up a full point.

Lester, Dini, Vargo, Clarissa, Raquel, and Ashton were all seated, and Mrs. Samuels was in the place of honor at the high table that let her look down on the rest of the diners.

I was just dishing out another bowl of soup when I felt the air go out of the room. I turned around.

Farrah stood nervously in the doorway to the home ec room. Her hair was pulled off her face and her cheeks were flushed.

It looked like she was the only Defiled who would show. I was so glad to see her, I barely knew what to say, so I said, "Welcome. Would you like some fruit?" even though I was holding a bowl of soup.

Mrs. Samuels, who was busy smelling her soup and making notes in her book, looked over at Farrah. "Oh, hello, dear! Sherm, make sure you usher your guests in and sit them promptly."

I put a bowl of soup in front of an empty seat across the table from Lester and Dini and pulled the chair out for Farrah. She slowly walked over and sat down. I stole a look at the Trophies. Vargo was watching Farrah intently. Lester kept stealing looks at her too, and Dini stared from Lester to Farrah. But no one got up and left. No one said anything mean to her or hit her with a piece of cutlery. My plan was working!

Farrah stared down at her bowl.

"It's cauliflower soup," explained Rick. "But it's not as bad as you'd think."

Next thing I knew, Vargo stood and walked over to Farrah, who jumped up and backed away. My heart began to thump. Everyone at the table stopped breathing.

"Hi," said Vargo. "I'm really glad you're here."

Then Vargo did something amazing. She reached over and gave Farrah a hug. All was still for a moment, and then everyone started clapping. Cauliflower soup must also be some kind of powerful aphrodisiac!

That's when I noticed Dini was watching Lester watch Farrah. He was staring at her like she was a ghost. A second later, Dini got up and walked out of the room.

The complexity of dinner party interactions cannot be underestimated.

Everyone loved the soup. Mrs. Samuels called me over and said she couldn't taste the Brie or see any oysters. I said I decided to change the recipe at the last minute. She said all the great chefs kept refining their menus right up to the last possible minute.

Bennett asked for seconds. It was the first time I'd ever heard him speak before he was spoken to.

The only fly in the soup was that Vanessa hadn't shown up. I didn't expect Anna after all the trauma she'd gone through earlier this week, and since

Jayne was in the hospital I figured she'd be MIA, too. But Vanessa *had* to come! More signs with her name and picture went up again in the bathrooms the day after we removed the first ones. Everyone here knew that she was on the list. The whole point of the party was to undefile Vanessa. She needed to get hugged by a Trophy Wife or two. She needed to get hugged by me.

Mrs. Samuels gestured at me to clear the bowls. For some reason I wondered if my mom and Fred were making out at his place. I made a mental note to sneak up on them once I got done here. Then I went into the office to call Vanessa.

There was no answer at her house. When I was coming back down the hallway, I smelled something burning. The carrots had only started boiling a couple of minutes before. They couldn't have burned dry already. And the chicken and pasta were being warmed in the oven. I started to run. Mrs. Samuels would knock off major marks if I incinerated one of my dishes!

As soon as I came into the room, Mrs. Samuels said, "Sherman, you'd better start serving the main course. Your guests are getting giddy."

She meant Clarissa, who was drawing inappropriate pictures on the paper tablecloth and showing them to Rick, who was laughing and holding on to his stomach.

Then Mrs. Samuels sniffed the air like a bloodhound.

"Did you leave a burner on?"

Ashton got up from the table and walked toward the stove. "I do believe something's on fire," he said.

I ran past him. The carrots were steaming away. The dishes in the oven were warm. Nothing was on fire. But the smell of smoke was getting stronger.

I heard a shout from outside.

"What's going on here?" a man's voice bellowed.

We all ran to the window.

Lying on the lawn under the window of the home ec room was Vanessa. Underneath her was a small person. Coach Little stood over them.

A thick stream of black smoke poured off a sooty object lying near Vanessa and the person she was entangled with. An overturned gas can lay nearby.

"I got him!" she said.

I couldn't stop staring at the arsonist, whose face was shoved into the grass. There was something familiar about him.

It was his shoes. I knew those shoes!

"Ed?" I said.

HOW'S A GUY SUPPOSED
TO IMPRESS A GIRL?

By the time Coach Little had convinced Vanessa to get off Ed the Head we had all run outside, all of us except for Mrs. Samuels, who said, "Go, go! I'll watch the food."

"You want to explain this?" asked Coach Little, pointing at the burning thing, which turned out to be a smoldering piece of wood.

"Has anyone called the fire department yet?" asked Rick.

"What for?" asked Ashton.

"Well, for one thing, that brick is leaving scorch marks on the lawn," said Rick.

Ed still hadn't spoken. Vanessa had gotten up

and now stood with her foot on his back.

"It's him!" said Vanessa, her big brown eyes sparking with anger.

"Shut up, bitch," muttered Ed.

"What's him?" I asked.

"He's the Defiler. I caught him."

"Defiler?" said Coach Little.

No one said a word and Coach Little growled. "You kids keep an eye on him. I'm going to go call the principal."

"And the fire department?" said Rick.

Coach Little bent down and looked into Ed's face. "Don't even think about moving."

When Coach was gone, I said, "Ed?"

Vanessa took her foot off Ed's back and he sat up.

He looked at me. I'd always thought he was a burnout, but now I realized that wasn't it. His eyes weren't high. They were dead.

"Ed," he repeated. "Ed the Head."

We all stared.

"How'd you like to be called that? That's all I am to you losers. Least I'm not a Defiler. You want to see Defilers, look in the mirror."

He sounded like Farrah. I looked around. Where was Farrah, anyway? I didn't see her or Lester. Or Dini.

"What did any of those girls ever do to you?" asked Vargo.

"All you bitches liked me fine when I was younger. Then I stop growing and suddenly I don't exist. So I start selling weed and I'm the shit again. Screw you," said Ed, still speaking in a weird monotone.

"His middle name is Dee," said Vanessa. "Edward Dee Snider. Like that guy in the band Twisted Sister."

I was having a lot of trouble keeping up. So Ed's parents named him after an eighties hair metal band. They had poor judgment in names. I knew firsthand about parents like that.

"I went to see Jayne Manklow in the hospital. She told me she used to go out with Ed, who used to go by his middle name, Dee. She was convinced he had something to do with defiling her."

My head pounded. Vanessa caught the Defiler? That was supposed to be my job! I'd been on the case for weeks, getting my ass kicked and my bike stolen and peeing in people's yards while on stakeout. It didn't seem fair. On one hand, it was sort of hot that she caught him, but on the other hand, how's a guy supposed to impress a girl when she's more impressive than he is?

"So how'd you catch him?" I asked.

"Remember that day in cooking class? When you got the warning picture? Ed came in that day and mooched some food off one of the other groups. I didn't think anything of it at the time, but after Jayne told me that she dated him I started to wonder. So I started surveilling Ed."

"You hid outside his house?"

"Yeah, that's when I saw him heading over here with a gas can."

Ed laughed softly.

"You were going to burn some wood at us?" I said.

"I was going to throw it through the window. Like a Molotov cocktail. That would have been the end of your little dinner party. 'Cept the frickin' thing wouldn't stay lit. I guess it's green wood or something."

"Isn't that a little harsh?" I said.

Ed laughed again and then raised his dead eyes to mine.

"Look, kid, I nearly got that skank to off herself. I got four or five others to drop out of school. I got you and your little Anna friend beat up just this week. Your sad, burned asses would just be another stop on the Dee Tour."

"What did I ever do to you?" I asked. "What did *they* ever do to you?"

"You were getting all up in my business. I can't have that. I went out with Jayne since seventh grade. We hit high school and she starts dating Mr. Hockey Player. All of a sudden I'm too low-class for her. She starts pretending she doesn't even know me. Pretending she's not the biggest pothead around."

"But Jayne's mom said you helped her straighten out," I said.

"Moms are like teachers," said Ed. "They always get their shit backward. Here's this girl, been taking my friendly for free for all this time. So I say to myself, screw her. I go to put up her picture in the bathroom. I'm going to write a little something on it. Dee Did Her or something like that, but someone comes in and I only have time to write the *D* before I slapped it up there." Ed laughed, a small, mean sound. "Turns out that's all you vicious bastards needed. You were all just looking for an excuse to put her in her place. Stoner girl trying to move into the fast lane. Somebody said the *D* stood for defiled."

Ed looked from person to person.

"I'll tell you something. I never would have come up with something that sick. It worked. People started acting like she actually was defiled. They couldn't say enough bad things about her. The hockey player dumped her once he heard what a slut she was, even though I was her only boyfriend before him. Then some genius got the idea to start ignoring her. That was it. She really was defiled then. Thanks to you upstanding citizens."

"We didn't do that," said Vargo. She looked close to tears.

"You didn't do anything to stop it, either, did you? You didn't ask if the rumors about her or any of the other girls were true. You just went along. Hey, Vargo," said Ed, leaning in. "How many defiled girls have you talked to in the last couple of years?"

Vargo looked down.

"You pieces of shit think I'm just some burnout. You buy my product, and you do my bidding," he said, his eyes glittering now. "I got you to defile every girl who ever pissed me off. All I had to do was pick the right ones. Girls on the edge. Girls with shitty friends. None of you questioned it."

"Why Farrah?" I asked. "She's your cousin."

"I told her not to go out with Lester. Him and his fancy hair and his pimped-out ride. I told her he wouldn't stand by her. I was right, too. Soon as I put her on the wall he was gone." Ed looked at each of us in turn.

"The question you should ask yourselves is, who fixed those other girls?"

"What other girls?" I asked.

"I didn't do the last two."

42

KEEPING THE LOSERS IN LINE

After Coach Little hauled Ed off, the rest of us stood around. We didn't know quite what to do.

Vargo and Clarissa and Raquel looked at each other. I looked at Vanessa. Rick and Ashton looked at the girls. Bennett looked at the horizon.

"Let's eat," I said, remembering the food.

Considering how long it had been warming in the oven, the chicken and the pasta weren't half bad. Even the carrots were fine. I'd just finished serving Mrs. Samuels when a flash of movement outside caught my eye.

"Enjoy!" I said to Mrs. Samuels. "And excuse me!"

I went to the window. Lester was rolling around on the ground with a guy while a girl tried to pull them apart. The weird thing is that they were almost totally silent.

I went outside to get a closer look. Sitting, watching the fight, was Dini.

"It's Farrah's brother," she said. "He caught Lester and Farrah kissing in the parking lot. He chased Lester back here. Farrah's trying to break it up."

"Oh, man," I said. "You saw them, too?"

She nodded. "I was doing a little surveilling of my own."

What is it with these girls that when they surveil they see everything and when I surveil I see nothing?

"Are you okay?"

"His hair bugged me," she said. "I couldn't compete."

We watched Farrah try to pull her brother off Lester.

"Vanessa caught the Defiler," I said.

"Oh, yeah? Who was it?"

"Ed the Head. His real name is Edward Dee Snider."

"Good going, Vanessa," she said.

I snuck a look at her profile to see if I was still in love with her. I wasn't. I mean, I would always be a little bit in lust with her, but I was in lust with most every girl, so it didn't count.

"Should I break this up?" I asked, pointing at Lester and Farrah's brother.

"Could you?"

"Probably not."

"You want some food?" I asked.

"Sure," she said. I held out my hand and she took it and followed me back into the school.

I waited until everyone had finished dessert and was handing in their Meal & Experience Evaluation forms to Mrs. Samuels. I had no worries, really. Not to brag or anything, but I was pretty sure I'd hosted the most exciting dinner party this town has ever seen. Sure, Fred helped me out with the soup and the carrots and Dini cut up the fruit really nice and I got my recipes off the Internet, but I think it's important to be flexible. I'm going to get that soup recipe from Fred and make it myself sometime, so it's not totally cheating.

Clarissa and Vargo gave me another awesome two-girl hug and offered to help do the dishes. I told them it was okay, that Rick and Ashton would do them, but I had another favor to ask. I heard Ashton telling Dini that her fruit plate was one of the most beautiful he'd ever seen and he'd been exposed to a lot of fruit plates. Then she said that she thought the table setting was super cutting edge. They may be on the verge of dating. But I am okay with it. Like I said, my feelings have changed.

A few minutes later I asked Raquel into the hallway after she slid her evaluation under a few others.

"Hey," I said. "Can I talk to you for a minute over here?" I stood near the entrance to the boys' washroom.

Her perfect lips curled up into a smile. A smile no more real than the color of her highlights. She walked back toward me.

"I'm sorry, Sherman. I've really got to get going. Tal is waiting for me. If he finds out I've been here, you know, after those pictures of us, he'll lose it for sure. You wouldn't want that, would you?"

It was a threat.

"Why'd you do it?" I asked.

She pretended she didn't know what I was talking

about. "Do what?" she asked.

"Defile Vanessa. I already figured out why you defiled Anna."

"You're high," she said, her tongue flicking at the gloss on her lips.

"I don't get it. You're beautiful. You're popular. You have everything. Why would you do it?"

Raquel's face changed and she sneered at me.

"Anna was with Tal, wasn't she?" I said.

"Little slut. I heard about it from one of Tal's friends. How dare she touch my man?"

"Is that why you leaked those pictures of you kissing me? To get back at Tal?"

"He thinks he can dog around on me? Make out with ninth graders and I won't find out? Humiliate me?" Raquel's voice rose.

"Why beat me up? Why defile Vanessa?"

"Because, you twerp, I was sick of you sticking your nose in where it doesn't belong. I *like* defiling. It keeps the losers in line. You were trying to destroy it. I figured if your little girlfriend got defiled you'd lay off."

I shook my head.

"Don't shake your head at me. It's bad enough my girls think you're cute. It won't last. They're fickle. You're a joke to them. You're nobody in this school. Nothing. Even if you stop defiling, you still won't be popular."

She paused for a long second and shook out her hair.

"Anyway, you can't prove any of this."

"He doesn't have to," said Vargo and Clarissa as they walked out of the boys' washroom, where I'd asked them to wait and listen.

The smirk fell from Raquel's beautiful face, leaving it blank.

"You're a disgrace," said Vargo.

"But we're—"

"Don't even say 'Trophy Wives,'" said Clarissa. "You were always way too into that concept. It's insulting, dude."

And the two of them walked down the hallway and through the front doors, leaving Raquel staring openmouthed after them. I went to rejoin my friends where they were cleaning up the home ec room.

ALL I EVER WANTED

After a person's been working a hot case, it can be tough to relax. So I decided to do what most investigators do and write up a conclusion. Here it is: Raquel's not a Trophy Wife anymore. She's not even a wife, because Tal Manhas dumped her. Last I heard, she was transferring to a school in the north end.

How did I know she was the other Defiler? Well, Raquel liked controlling people. She liked manipulating situations. And she was wicked competitive and jealous. Like I said, I'm kind of a scholar of women.

Ed is expelled forever for attempted arson, and since the cops found serious weight in his locker he may end up doing time. It turns out he's eighteen.

He's not even much taller than me. I feel for him, I really do.

There are no more defiled people at Harewood Tech. Sure, there are people who get picked on. Guys who get kicked around. Girls who no one likes. But no one is invisible. Except those of us in ninth grade. We're still mostly invisible.

Anna came back to school. She's turned Goth. She's now the most Goth of them all. It suits her.

And my love life? Well, Vanessa and I have this new connection. After the cops asked her a few questions and then took Ed away she stuck around and helped us clean up. And later when I walked her home she kissed me. Just a little one on the cheek, but still. She's gone back to talking to me like I'm not too smart, but sometimes I catch her looking at me. She feels something. I know she does.

My dinner party made me sort of famous around school. Not many guys have had the chance to feed a complete set of Trophy Wives, especially guys my age. Dudes have been coming up to me asking for advice on dating. I heard enrollment in cooking class has doubled for next term and Mrs. Samuels has more applications for the Cafeteria

Program than she can take.

Which reminds me that I got an A on my project, even though the food was a little lukewarm and I couldn't keep the guests at the table for more than five minutes because of everything going on around us.

"Welcome to Cafeteria," said Mrs. Samuels, handing me my final comments from her and the rest of the guests.

"Thanks, Mrs. S.," I said.

She handed me one evaluation form separately.

"I left this one out. Some diners you just can't please."

It was Raquel's form. She didn't like my dinner. She wrote that my chicken Parmesan tasted like donkey ass, which was rude and also untrue.

My mom and Fred are sort of dating. Probably because of all that time they spent together waiting for my dinner to be over. It could be worse. Fred's a decent guy. I just don't think people's mothers should date. That's all.

Most interesting of all, I seem to have developed a rep as an investigator. People have been coming up to me asking for help locating people and finding out who said what about them. It's a lot to take in. I haven't taken on any new cases yet. I'm waiting for the right one.

And Dini, the girl who started it all? She and Ashton have gone out a few times. They spent one afternoon painting the skateboarders in the skate park and another afternoon painting each other's portraits onto an overpass. She always smiles when she sees me. This afternoon I saw Farrah sitting with Lester in his car. It looked like they were arguing, but when she saw me, she smiled. Then, later, Vanessa smiled at me when I walked into cooking class.

Here's a Mack Daddy insight: I think that girls smiling at me when I walk into the room is all I've ever wanted.